*"Live the magic,"*

Jorgie hadn't realized Quint had been inching his body closer, but now she felt his thigh pressed against hers and his hand had slipped from her shoulders to her waist. He was reaching up with his other hand to gently stroke her cheek.

He gazed into her eyes. He was going to kiss her. She should move. But Jorgie was caught up in the moment. By the singing gondolier, by the Grand Canal, by the full moon rising over the Venetian sky, by the dark water and the summer breeze and Quint, Quint, Quint.

Slowly she closed her eyes, puckered her lips and waited. And when his mouth touched hers, she understood the true appeal of Casanova.

He made a woman feel cherished and adored.

Dear Reader,

Did you ever have a schoolgirl crush on the cute older guy in your neighborhood? Do you remember the way your heart beat faster whenever you caught a glimpse of him mowing his lawn without a shirt on? And how you spent those long summer nights imagining he was trailing his calloused masculine fingers over your tender feminine flesh? Well, Jorgie Gerard sure did, even though she'd almost forgotten about her teenage infatuation with Quint Mason. That is, until she runs into him in the airport on her way to an erotic, adults-only vacation in Venice, Italy.

What Jorgie doesn't realize is that Quint has fond memories of her, as well. Nor does she know that he's really an undercover agent on his way to the same resort destination, posing as a guest lecturer and expert on Casanova in order to catch a criminal. By day he does his job, but by night...oh, the heat of the wicked Venetian evenings spent alone with Jorgie... Quint is beginning to realize this could very well be his last seduction.

I hope you enjoy *His Final Seduction.* Visit my Web site, www.loriwilde.com, for news on upcoming books and more!

Happy reading,

Lori Wilde

# Lori Wilde

## HIS FINAL SEDUCTION

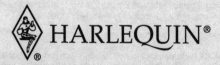

HARLEQUIN®

TORONTO • NEW YORK • LONDON
AMSTERDAM • PARIS • SYDNEY • HAMBURG
STOCKHOLM • ATHENS • TOKYO • MILAN • MADRID
PRAGUE • WARSAW • BUDAPEST • AUCKLAND

Recycling programs
for this product may
not exist in your area.

ISBN-13: 978-0-373-79522-2

HIS FINAL SEDUCTION

**Printed in U.S.A.**

## ABOUT THE AUTHOR

Lori Wilde is the author of forty books. She's been nominated for a RITA® Award and four *RT Book Reviews* Reviewers' Choice Awards. Her books have been excerpted in *Cosmopolitan, Redbook* and *Quick & Simple.* Lori teaches writing online through Ed2go. She's also an R.N. trained in forensics, and volunteers at a women's shelter. Visit her Web site at www.loriwilde.com.

## Books by Lori Wilde

To the staff at eHarlequin, who all work so hard to get the word out about our books.

# *1*

*Something Sexy in the Air*
—Eros Airlines

SEX HAD NEVER LOOKED so intriguing.

Or so scary.

*That's precisely the point. You need to step outside your comfort zone.*

Jorgina Gerard closed the glossy brochure, featuring Eros Airlines and Fantasy Resort erotic vacation packages, and fanned herself with it. She was alarmed that her body was suddenly aroused at—of all places—the Dallas/Fort Worth International Airport ticket kiosk. Mentally, she gave herself a shake. What was the matter with her?

*Um, could it be because you haven't had sex since your boyfriend dumped you?*

Cringing, Jorgie bit down on her bottom lip. All around her there was bustling activity—business travelers rolling their carry-on bags toward the taxi stands, separated lovers reuniting with heartfelt hugs, harried moms and dads herding ebullient children away from the enticing dangers of escalators and baggage carousels.

What was she doing? Why had she let her best friend since kindergarten, Avery Bodel, talk her into this? Was she insane? Embarking on an exotic itinerary dubbed with the provocative title Make Love Like A Courtesan. She didn't need sex lessons. She was twenty-five. She watched cable television. She'd been in a serious relationship and…and…

And as Brian had walked out the door he'd tossed the accusation over his shoulder. "You're just too damned conventional in the sack, Jorgina. Men need variety, excitement, danger."

Danger? Jorgie closed her eyes and took a deep breath. Maybe she wasn't the problem, maybe it was Brian.

And if Brian was the problem, then she didn't need to be here, right? She just needed to find some guy who could appreciate conventional.

"You know," she began, turning to her friend. This week, Avery's hair was dyed the color of muscat grapes—a deep hue of acrid purple. As a hairdresser, Avery changed her hair style and color as often as most people changed clothes. "Maybe this—"

"Oh, no," said Avery. She wrapped a restraining hand around Jorgie's wrist. "You are not!"

"Not what?" Jorgie asked, but her voice came out high and squeaky, giving her away.

"You're not fooling me. I've known you too long. You've got that I'm-gonna-run-away-from-fun look in your eyes. Same look you had in eighth grade when we played Spin The Bottle at Miley Kinslow's birthday party and it pointed to the guy you'd been mooning over."

"Quint Mason," Jorgie supplied, wondering if he liked conventional girls.

She'd had a puppy-love crush on Quint for the entire school year and he barely knew she existed. If she squeezed her eyes closed tightly enough, she could still see him as he'd looked then—lanky, medium brown hair, a devilish grin that melted tweenaged hearts. Of course as a tenth grader, he'd never given her the time of day and she'd been far too shy to even say boo to him, but she'd been besotted. Jorgie sighed. She'd been getting it wrong with the opposite sex ever since.

Wonder what ever happened to him? Then she remembered something her brother Keith had told her in passing after his ten-year high school reunion the previous fall. He'd heard Quint had been stationed in Afghanistan, but that he'd recently left the air force and was working for some private airline. That did not sound like a conventional guy.

"Yeah." Avery tapped her temple with an index finger. "Quint Mason. That's him. This trip is just like that. You have the chance to grab life by the throat and really live."

"But is an erotic destination vacation really the answer?"

"Look at this." Avery snatched the Eros brochure from her hand and shook it under her nose. "Look at all the opportunities you'd be running away from." Her friend flipped through the pages, reading the copy as she went. "Learn the sex secrets every courtesan knew. Find out how to hold men completely in your thrall. Dance the seductive dance that brought kings to their knees. Become an exotic woman of pleasure."

Embarrassment heated Jorgie's cheeks. She snatched the brochure back and stuffed it inside her purse. "Shh, someone will hear you."

Avery shrugged. "So what? I'm not ashamed."

"There are kids around."

"Hey, I'm not their mother. It's not my job to censor their exposure to life."

"Maybe not, but you don't have to announce to the entire airport where we're going."

"Seriously," Avery said, "don't run away. This is your chance to show that dork Brian that you're anything but conventional. And where does he get off calling you conventional? You two met at an accountants' conference, for crying out loud. He's just as conventional as you, or he was before he—"

"But I *am* conventional."

"Conventional is as conventional does."

"Huh?"

"It's something my grammie says."

"Your grammie says 'conventional is as conventional does'?"

"No, she says 'pretty is as pretty does,' I just substituted *conventional,* but the advice still applies."

"It doesn't make sense either way."

"Sure it does. Act pretty and you'll be pretty. Act conventional and you'll be conventional. Act unconventional and—"

"I get your drift."

"So stop having cold feet. Actually, stop thinking. You think too much, Jorgie."

"And you don't ever look before you leap, Avery."

"But I have a lot more fun than you do."

Jorgie sighed. True enough. "You know this is just a variation of the same conversation we've been having for twenty years."

"I'm the accelerator…" Avery said, starting the quote their mothers spoke over their heads as they'd played in the sandbox together. Avery was the kid who flung herself headfirst down the slide. While Jorgie was the crying girl who hovered on the top rung of the ladder, too scared to climb back down, too fearful to take the plunge.

"And I'm the brake," Jorgie finished.

"We balance each other out. It's the secret to our lifelong friendship." Grinning, Avery slung her arm over Jorgie's shoulder.

Avery's grin bolstered her sagging confidence. The truth was, she didn't know what she'd do without her. Avery had such a life force. Whenever she was around her, Jorgie felt stronger, braver, more adventuresome. What few risks Jorgie had taken were due solely to her best friend's influence. Avery was like an exuberant leader, barreling her way through life on her magnetic charm and sheer good luck.

"Your turn." Avery elbowed her forward.

Shoulder muscles tensed tight as a wire, Jorgie stepped up to the kiosk and inserted her credit card. *Ready or not, this was going down.*

"While you're doing that," Avery told her, "I'm going up to the ticket counter."

"Huh? What for?"

"Never you mind. I'll be right back." Avery raised her hand over her head and gave Jorgie a backward wave. She sashayed over to the ticket counter, her low-slung jeans and cropped cotton T-shirt revealing a peek at the vivid ink art decorating her lower spine. Jorgie would never ever have the courage to get a tattoo, but as much as Avery's audacity shocked her, she also admired it.

The ticket kiosk spit out Jorgie's boarding pass.

It was confirmed. She and Avery were on their way to Venice to learn how to make love like courtesans. Not that Avery needed sex lessons—the woman kept more men dangling on the string than she could count—but her friend could definitely do with a dose of the courtesans' famed discretion.

Okay, all right, she would do this. She needed this. It

was time she stopped playing it safe. Brian was right. She *was* too conventional. She could do this as long as she had Avery beside her.

Speaking of Avery, where in the heck had she gotten to?

Ticket in one hand and her carry-on clasped in the other, Jorgie spun away from the kiosk. She was so busy searching the crowd for her friend that she didn't see the man barreling down on her until it was too late. She tried to zigzag, but that only made things worse.

*Wham!*

They collided in a tangle of arms and legs and rolling leather luggage.

"Miss, are you okay?" His voice was as deep as Phantom Lake, where her parents owned a summer cottage.

His hands were on her shoulders, steadying her. That's when Jorgie realized she was on the floor and her skirt had flipped up, revealing way too much of her thighs. She yanked her skirt to her knees and darted her gaze to his face. Had he noticed?

The slick, knowing grin said, oh, yeah, he'd noticed.

And she was noticing for the first time just how extremely handsome he was. The stuff of daydreams. Chiseled jaw. Neatly trimmed thick, wavy brown hair. Mischievous cocoa-colored eyes. A slightly crooked nose that told her it had been broken at one time, but that kept him from being too damned gorgeous.

She felt like fleeing. Jorgie gulped, stared. *Say something, dummy.*

"Hey," he said. "Don't I know you?"

It surprised her that he'd use such a tired line. He looked as if he would know all the cutting-edge come-ons. She frowned, shook her head, unable to speak against the weight of his warm, distracting hand upon her shoulder.

"Yeah, yeah, sure I do. I used to hang out with your brother Keith, when my family lived in Burleson. It's Quint, Quint Mason. Remember me?" He extended a hand.

Quint Mason? Was it possible? Here? Now? She stared, stunned by coincidence and the power of his presence.

His hand stayed outstretched, the smile firmly hung on his lips.

She almost laughed. Not because there was anything funny, but to help relieve her nervous tension. What else could she do? She had to accept his help.

His hand was warm and hard and friendly, just like the man himself. Gently, he tugged her to her feet.

She felt oddly absurd, as if she'd stumbled down an *Alice in Wonderland* rabbit hole. "Umm…umm…" she stammered.

"Janie, is it? No, wait…" He snapped his fingers. "Jorgie. It's Jorgie, right?"

Happiness flowed over her. Mutely, she nodded. He'd remembered her name.

"You've changed," he said, giving her the once-over with an appreciative light dancing in his eyes. She wasn't the only one who'd changed. He'd gone from lean and lanky to muscular and broad-shouldered. "No more braces."

Her body flushed hot at his appraisal. "I got them off when I was a sophomore."

"No more pigtails." His hand went to her hair, his fingertips briefly skimming her neck.

Goose bumps set up camp on her forearms, and her breathing grew so shallow she was practically panting. "Left those behind with the private school uniform," she managed to say.

"You don't have library books clutched in your arms. Did you lose your love of reading?"

"Nope. Nothing's changed there, but I've upgraded to an e-book reader. Got it stashed in my purse for the plane ride."

"And you lost the glasses. LASIK or contact lenses?"

"LASIK," she said.

"Me, too."

"It's amazing you recognized me at all."

"Those eyes are the same." He nodded as if speaking the wisdom of the ages. "So deep blue that they're almost purple. Like a Colorado mountain stream. Not many people in the world have eyes like that. The minute I looked into them, I knew it was you."

*He remembered her.*

She shouldn't have found the idea so thrilling, but she did. Her junior high crush remembered her. Her heart did a crazy little rumba.

*Oh, just stop it. You're being silly.*

"You know," he said. "I'd love to stop and talk. Catch up on old times…"

What old times? She hadn't spoken ten words to him the entire year he'd lived in Burleson and hung out with her brother. She'd been far too shy.

"Find out what Keith is up to these days, but…" He glanced at his watch. "I'm late for work. Maybe we could hook up later." His comment had been mildly made, but it threw her off to think of meeting up with him again.

"Maybe." She breathed hopefully even as her brain churned cruel taunts. *Get a grip. He's not interested in you. He's just being polite. Why would a guy like him be interested in you? He's traveled the world over. Been in the military. Probably been with dozens—maybe even hundreds—of women. He's seen and done things you could never dream of. You could never hold the attention of a guy like that. If you couldn't hold on to someone as bland as Brian, you don't have a prayer with Quint.*

He pulled a card from the pocket of his houndstooth sport jacket—he just had to be a snappy dresser, as well as good-looking—and passed it over to her. "Give me a call when you get back in town."

Yeah, right. She'd find the courage to do that about the same time hell froze over. Still, she palmed the card, clutched it tight.

"See ya." He picked up his carry-on, raised a hand in farewell and took off.

Stunned, Jorgie felt as if she'd been clipped in a drive-by. What was that?

"Omigod, who's the hottie?" Avery asked as she sidled up to Jorgie. Simultaneously, they both cocked their heads to watch Quint walk away, the fabric of his slacks molding to his butt. They sighed in unison.

"That," Jorgie explained, "was Quint Mason."

"Quint Mason of Spin The Bottle fame? Get outta town." Avery gave her a playful shove.

Jorgie pointed to her luggage. "I'm working on it."

Avery giggled. "You know what I mean. This is incredible."

"How so?"

"Seriously. It's kismet, fate, serendipity. I mean we were just talking about him and *poof*…here he is. What are the odds?"

"Well, actually," Jorgie said, her mathematical accountant's mind kicking in, "the probability isn't as slim as you might think, given that Quint works in the airline industry and DFW is the biggest airport in the state. He probably passes through here every morning on his way to work."

"Yeah, but what are the odds that you'd be standing here when he sauntered by?"

"I could do a statistical analysis if you wanted…"

Avery plastered her palms over both ears. "No, no, please spare me. Numbers make my head explode."

"It's really just like that phenomena where you decide to buy a certain kind of car—"

"Spyder, I want a Spyder."

"You decide to buy a Spyder," Jorgie played along, "and suddenly everywhere you look the place is crawling with Spyders."

"Pun intended?"

"You know me. I can't resist wordplay."

"You can't resist anything brainiacish."

"Anyway…" Jorgie ignored that comment. "If we hadn't been talking about Quint, then I probably would never have noticed him. He would have walked right on by. Just like if you weren't dying to own a Spyder, you wouldn't notice every single one of them that drove past."

"Except that he didn't walk right on by, he ran smack-dab into you."

"You saw that?"

"The whole airport saw it."

Jorgie winced. She hated being the center of attention and nothing embarrassed her more than public humiliation. Unlike Avery, who courted the spotlight with glee.

"Don't obsess about it," Avery said, accurately reading her. "No one cares that your skirt was practically up around your waist."

Jorgie groaned.

"Look at the bright side. At least you don't wear thongs. Come on. Let's get through security before the line gets any longer. Our plane starts boarding in fifteen minutes."

Avery was right. No point obsessing over something she couldn't change. She needed to live in the moment. Get fired up about her trip. She was going to Venice. What more could a woman ask for?

By the time they were through the checkpoint and found their gate at Eros Air, boarding was already in progress.

"Hey," Avery said, nudging Jorgie in the side. "Isn't that your guy?"

"What guy?"

"Mr. Handsome over there by the gate attendant."

Jorgie focused on the jetway. Sure enough, it was Quint Mason getting on the plane. Her plane. To Venice. What was he doing on her plane? Quint had said he was late for work. Did he work for Eros? Was he a pilot, or a navigator, or a flight attendant? But he wasn't in uniform.

Jorgie frowned and looked at her ticket. "Are we at the right gate?"

"E37. That's you."

She focused back on Avery. "What do you mean, that's me?"

"This is your gate."

"My gate?" She raised an eyebrow.

Avery shifted her weight. "My gate's at E34."

"Your gate?" She sounded like a parrot.

"I decided at the last minute I'd rather go on the Make Love Like A Movie Star tour. I'm going to Hollywood."

Avery's statement shocked her so much Jorgie didn't immediately register what she'd said. "Huh?"

"I'm going to Hollywood," she repeated.

"That's what you were doing at the ticket counter? Changing your destination?"

Avery had the good grace to look ashamed. "Yes."

"And they just let you switch like that?"

"I had to pay a fee, but, yeah."

Jorgie felt as if she'd been slapped across the face. "What's going on? Why didn't you tell me? I would be just as happy going on the movie star tour. Let's go back and swap my ticket over."

"Um, I kinda, sorta, wanted to go alone."

Dismay sucked all the anticipation out of her. "But…but…" Jorgie sputtered. "This whole Eros vacation was your idea. You told me to spread my wings, to claim my sexuality and show Brian that I could be as unconventional as…as…"

Avery placed a hand on Jorgie's shoulder. "And that's what you're going to do."

"Not without you I'm not."

"Jorg, we've gotta cut the cord sometime. I can't keep being your id. You gotta learn how to develop your own sense of fun."

"Well, that sounds all great and everything," Jorgie said, still stunned by the turn of events. She'd never expected Avery to pull something like this. Sure, her friend was spontaneous and free-spirited and, okay, she could be irresponsible at times, but she'd never betrayed Jorgie before. "But who's going to be your brake?"

"That's just it. This time, I wanna freefall. No brakes, no parachutes, nothing to hold me back."

Jorgie gaped openmouthed. "I…I…never knew you felt this way. I thought we balanced each other out. I thought that was why our friendship worked so well."

"Listen, it's not the end of the world," Avery said in a perky voice as if she wasn't about to cut the cord with a pair of giant metaphorical scissors. "We're simply taking separate vacations."

"I would never have agreed to the trip if I'd known you were going to bail on me." Jorgie fisted her hands.

"I know." Avery smiled. "It's the reason I had to pull a stunt like this. I hope you'll forgive me for the subterfuge."

Betrayal had an ugly taste, bitter and hard. "Don't do this. You can switch your ticket back. I'll pay for the fee. Please."

"Time to pull up your big-girl panties, Jorgie." Avery hoisted her knapsack onto her shoulder. "Ciao."

"You can't… You're not… Avery, don't leave me."

"You're too dependent on me, kiddo."

Her friend was right. She sounded so desperate. She felt desperate, too. Her life had been unraveling ever since Brian left her and now Avery was leaving her, too. "Please…"

"You can do this. I have faith. We'll call each other every day and share our experiences."

"Ave…" Jorgie was finding it hard to breathe. A tumult of emotions clogged her lungs. She felt scared and betrayed and angry and, strangely enough, just a little bit excited. She'd never done anything on her own. She and Avery had roomed together in college, and then afterward she'd met Brian and they'd moved in together. Then after Brian had left, Avery rented Jorgie's spare bedroom. She'd never lived alone. Never traveled alone.

"Final boarding call for Eros Air flight 692," said a voice over the loudspeaker.

"Go on." Avery gave her a gentle shove toward the jetway. "This is for your own good."

"I…"

"Spread your wings, Jorgie. Flout convention. Fly. Go to your destiny." Then with that parting advice, Avery turned and scurried away. Quickly, the crowd swallowed her up.

Jorgie stood frozen, her heart pounding madly. The gate agent looked at her expectantly, hand outstretched to receive her boarding pass.

She locked eyes with the woman and the life-changing events of the last few weeks washed over her. Getting dumped by Brian for essentially being too timid, getting passed over for a promotion at work because she wasn't aggressive enough (a direct quote from her boss), the decision to take Avery's advice and sign up for an erotic fantasy vacation, unexpectedly meeting Quint Mason and then discovering he was on her flight. Was it kismet? Was serendipity at work here? Had the universe converged to plant her in this spot at this time under these conditions for a reason?

Jorgie wasn't fanciful. She was an accountant. A cruncher of numbers. She liked things that made sense, and this romantic notion of destiny defied logic. And yet, here she was with the cosmic dominoes all lined up. Did she have the courage to knock them down?

"Miss?" the gate agent asked. "Are you boarding?"

It was now or never. Time to prove she could be bold and daring, or forever accept her fate as a shy, conventional woman who could never attract the attention of someone like, say…Quint Mason.

Jorgie raised her chin and slapped her ticket into the gate agent's hand. "Yes," she said. "Yes, I am."

# 2

*Keep your heart unfettered and your fingers nimble*
*—Make Love Like Casanova*

WELL, WELL, WELL, little Jorgie Gerard had grown up quite nicely.

From his seat in the back of the plane, Quint Mason watched her board the Eros Air Bombardier CRJ200. She moved up the aisle, her carry-on bag clutched in her hand. His gaze tripped lightly over her lush curves. She hadn't possessed a body like that thirteen years ago. He would have remembered.

Spellbound, he simply stared. The front of her silky, powder-blue blouse dipped, revealing just a hint of cleavage, but it was enough to cause instant sweat to bead on the back of his neck in the confines of the expensively decorated aircraft. She stopped a few rows ahead of him and looked down to double-check her seat assignment, and then she looked up again.

A ray of sunshine slanted through the open portal window, casting her in a bright surreal splash of yellow. For a whisper of a second, he could have sworn he heard harp music and the sound of angels singing. The woman who used to be his best friend's shy little sister was bathed in a whole new light.

Her straight, chestnut-brown hair—swept back off her neck in a demure ponytail—glinted with red highlights. His fingers itched to reach up and pull that band from her hair and watch it tumble about her shoulders. She wore a knee-length skirt that was a darker shade of blue than her blouse and blue, matching sandals decorated with pink flowers. She looked like exactly what she was—the girl-next-door all grown up. The kind you took home to meet your parents. Marriage material. He'd do well to steer clear.

But even as the light shifted, dimmed, Quint couldn't take his eyes off her and he didn't know why.

*Familiarity. She reminds you of a simpler time. That's all. A missive from your past.*

Still, his heart skipped a beat. That was odd. Usually the only time his heart misfired was when he drove his Corvette too fast or danced the tango or made love all night long. She was pretty, hell yeah, but certainly nothing extraordinary. Nothing to make him feel like this.

Still, there was something about the way she carried herself that clutched his gut and narrowed his focus to only her. She possessed a quality that called to something primal inside him. One thought snapped through his head hot as electricity.

*Gotta have her.*

Stupid, that impulse. It could lead nowhere but to big trouble. Quint lowered his eyelids, smiled slowly.

She sucked in her breath. He heard it all the way down the aisle. Quickly, she turned, reached for the overhead bin. In this private jet the bins were more lavish than on commercial liners, but she struggled to get her suitcase stuffed in.

Quint hopped from his seat. In one long-legged stride he was beside her. "Here, let me help you with that."

For a second, she looked as if she might argue with him, but when he reached for the handle, she let go just as his fingers touched hers. He caught a whiff of her delicate perfume. And he was jonesing for something sweet.

"Thank you," she whispered, her voice soft as a caress.

He was aware of a humming noise inside his brain, fraught with sexual energy. He stared at her lips, full and pink and shiny with gloss. His heart skipped another beat. What was the deal here? Was he developing a heart condition?

Frowning, Quint ripped his gaze from her distracting lips and fell into the pool of her deep blue eyes. He just stood there staring, her suitcase raised over his head, the bag braced against the cargo bin and his forearms.

*Snap out of it, Mason.* A woman hadn't left him this thunderstruck since high school.

"Is there a problem?" She lifted a hand to push back a tendril of hair from her face, the pink bracelets at her wrist jangling as they brushed against each other.

"Um…" *Do something, don't just stand there.* The aisle was clogging up behind her. Immediate, he shoved her suitcase into the overhead bin and clicked it closed.

"Thank you," she said, then sat down and snapped on her seat belt. She picked up the in-flight magazine and started flipping through it.

Not knowing what else do, he mumbled, "You're welcome," and went back to his seat.

Still feeling a bit off balance by the intensity of his attraction, Quint settled into his seat and mentally pried his mind off Jorgie and put it where it belonged.

On his job.

He was an air marshal on private security detail for the Lockhart Agency. For the last ten weeks, he and his fellow air marshals had been on assignment for Eros Airlines and Fantasy Adventure Vacations. The company's catchphrase was Something Sexy In The Air, and they specialized in catering to a high-end clientele that didn't mind spending money indulging their passionate sides.

But over the course of the past several months, the airline's owner, Taylor Milton, had gotten anonymous threatening letters at the same time someone had been sabotaging her four international resorts. She'd been reluctant to take her problems to the police and risk adverse publicity. To keep things discreet, she'd hired the Lockhart Agency to protect her interests.

The air marshals were undercover, both on the planes and at the resorts. Quint's cover identity was an instructor at the Venetian resort, teaching a daily course in How To Make Love Like Casanova. This was his third stint at the assignment. Quint had to admit he'd had a helluva good time, instructing men on how to be great lovers and flirting with the ladies to show off his skills. The only major drawback to the setup was the morality clause he'd been obligated to sign. No sex with the guests. For a sensualist like Quint, that was something of a challenge.

The sabotages had been fairly minor, mere inconveniences than anything else, until a month ago when someone had planted a small bomb at the Tokyo resort. The bomb had been found, the resort vacated and the explosive neutralized with no harm done, but clearly, the situation had escalated. Taylor Milton had beefed up security at the resorts and ever since then, there'd been no new occurrences and the threatening letters had stopped. It was eerie, waiting for the other shoe to drop.

Quint noticed no one took the seat beside Jorgie, but otherwise, the plane was full. Once they were airborne, he sent a text to his coworker Jake Stewart, who was at this very moment boarding a plane to Los Angeles for Eros's Make Love Like A Movie Star tour.

Any lookers? he typed into his BlackBerry.

Is that all you think about? Jake returned his text.

Quint laughed. Pretty much.

Casanova fits you to a T.

Get back on the horse, man. Jake had been divorced for over a year and as far as Quint knew he hadn't dated. He'd been bugging him to let loose and just have a fling, but Jake was one of those Dudley Do-Right types who never broke the rules.

Two words, Jake texted back. Morality Clause.

So, any lookers?

Yeah.

That took him by surprise. Quint smiled. Yeah?

Not my type.

All the better.

Door's closing. Later.

Chuckling, Quint put his BlackBerry away. The flight attendant was distributing drinks and he heard Jorgie order a Bloody Mary. After she'd been served her drink, he took the bottle of water the attendant gave him and slipped into the seat beside her. "Rough night?"

She looked startled to see him.

He nodded at her drink. "A Bloody Mary is a common hangover cure."

"No." She shook her head. "In fact, I rarely drink…"

"Fear of flying?"

"Not at all."

"The mystery deepens. You don't seem the type to drink alcohol at nine in the morning."

"Precisely."

"I'm not following you."

"I'm doing things I wouldn't normally do."

"Ah." He nodded. "Bad breakup."

"How do you know that?"

"You're traveling alone and drinking Bloody Marys and headed to an Eros resort. Common cure for a bad breakup."

"So you're saying I'm a cliché?"

He shrugged, grinned.

"I wasn't meant to be traveling alone. Actually my friend Avery was supposed to come with me, but at the last minute she changed her ticket, hopped on a plane to another Eros resort, leaving me holding the bag. I think I'm due for a Bloody Mary, don't you?"

"Drink up. I'll order you another."

She looked at the water bottle in his hand. "You're not drinking?"

"Not in the mood." He kept grinning. "But you go right ahead."

"That grin gets you laid a lot, doesn't it?"

Whoa, he hadn't expected that from the girl next door. His admiration shot up a notch. "I do all right."

"You haven't changed a bit since high school."

"It doesn't sound like a compliment the way you say it."

"What's not complimentary about being a twenty-nine-old man with a high school mentality?"

"Ouch, kitten. Withdraw the claws. I'm not the guy who done you wrong."

"No, but you're the one who decided to sit here. Better be prepared to take a little mortar fire or head back to where you came from."

This was getting really interesting. Quint leaned back

in his seat, buckled up his seat belt. He could do his job just as easily sitting here as in the last row. "It's a long flight and I'm all ears."

"You ever been engaged, Quint?" A disgruntled expression crossed her face and he found himself wishing he could hunt down the ex-boyfriend who'd dumped her and punch him out.

"Nope."

"Ever come close?"

"Nope."

"Ever want to get married?"

"Never crossed my mind."

She took a sip of her Bloody Mary, pointed a finger at him. "Smart man."

"So," he said, quickly changing the subject. "How's Keith? I saw him at our ten-year high school reunion and we had a few drinks. Shot the breeze, but we haven't kept in touch since then."

"Keith just got married, and he and his wife are expecting a baby girl in the fall."

"No kidding. But he's only…"

"Twenty-nine, same age as you."

"Seems too young to be tied down."

"He's really happy."

"Good for Keith." A wistfulness swept over him. It seemed all his buddies were getting married, settling down. He didn't get it. There was so much living to be done. You could get married and grow old anytime. But you were only young once.

"How's your parents?"

"They decided to follow their bliss and moved to Santa Fe. Mom runs an art gallery. Dad takes tourists on guided deer hunts."

"And your brother?"

"Gordy's still in the air force. He's gonna be just like Dad. Career military."

"But not you?"

"Naw. I've never been much for having other people tell me what to do. The service wasn't a natural fit. How about your parents?"

"They finally sold the house on Janie Lane, moved into a condo in downtown Fort Worth."

"You're kidding me."

"After years of suburban living, they said they wanted to be where the action is."

"I'm impressed. Paula and James living it up in Sundance Square."

"Things change," she said.

He raked his gaze over her, couldn't stop himself from taking in the swell of her breasts beneath her blouse. "Yeah, they do. What are you up to these days? Keith told me you worked for a big accounting firm and that you'd gotten your CPA."

"Still there."

"Is it the only job you've ever had?"

"Other than working at Six Flags when I was sixteen."

"Hey, Keith and I worked there one summer. At the ice cream emporium."

"I remember. You got fired for giving free banana splits to pretty girls."

"That memory of yours…" Quint shook his head, grinned. "It's wicked dangerous."

Their gazes locked and that same compelling zap that he'd felt when he bumped into her in the airport flashed through him again. What was this sudden, unexpected chemistry? She wasn't the type he normally went for. He liked tall, supergorgeous, sleek blondes with legs to the ceiling and more boobs than brains. Jorgie was nothing like that.

"Tell me, what is it that you do?" she asked. "When you flattened me in the terminal you said you were late for work. I thought you must be a pilot or flight attendant or something."

"I work for Eros," he said.

She eyed him. "In what capacity?"

"I'm an instructor."

An eyebrow rose on her forehead as if she didn't believe him. "What kind of instructor? I never figure you for the professorial type."

"I teach How To Make Love Like Casanova. The male counterpart to How To Make Love Like A Courtesan."

Jorgie almost choked on her Bloody Mary. "You're serious?"

"Yep."

"What do you teach them?"

"The art of seduction."

She giggled.

"Hey, it's not that funny." He pretended to look hurt. Hell, if a guy couldn't laugh at himself, who could he laugh it? The Casanova thing *was* pretty goofy.

"Are you practicing your skills on me now?" she asked.

"On an old friend?" He made a "no way" face and shook his head.

"Really?"

"Scout's honor." He held up two fingers of his left hand.

"Then how come you've got your elbow at the level of my breasts? You counting on an accidental boob graze?"

"What? You think I have no finesse?"

"You can stop trying to look affronted and move your elbow."

"You weren't this prickly when you were thirteen," he said, shifting his arm away from her breasts. He hadn't been angling for an accidental boob graze, but now that she'd brought it up, it was all he could think about. He was so aware of her. The air seemed to vibrate between them.

"You're incorrigible."

"What?"

"I see you staring at my breasts."

"And may I say what nice breasts they are?"

"Go on." She waved at him with both hands. "Shoo. Go back to your seat."

"You're kicking me out of your row?"

"I am."

"Heartless." He shook his head, gave her his best grin.

"Go." She pointed like he was a bad dog.

What had he done wrong? Quint wasn't accustomed to being shown the door. Women just naturally liked him and he liked them.

"You're serious?"

"Why do I get the feeling women rarely say no to you?"

"'Cause I know how to make love like Casanova?" He canted his head, tried his best to look adorable.

She snorted, rolled her eyes. "I've learned that guys who talk a good game usually do so in order to compensate for something." Then she very pointedly glanced at his crotch.

"Low blow. You really know how to hurt a guy, Jorgie."

"I bet you drive a sports car."

"I do."

"Let me guess, a heartbreaker red Corvette."

"How did you know?"

"Overcompensating."

"Ouch, ouch, ouch."

"Do you have gigantic speakers on your music system?"

"Huh?"

"The music system in your house. Do you have gigantic speakers?"

"I'm scared to answer that."

"I'll take it as a yes."

"Now I'm beginning to get a clue as to why your boyfriend bailed. You have no idea how to have fun." The minute he said it, Quint could have bitten off his tongue as the teasing light evaporated from her eyes. "I'm sorry," he amended. "That was out of line. I didn't mean it. You just had me on the ropes with the overcompensating thing and I came up swinging."

"It's okay," she said more cheerfully than he expected. "You're right. Brian left me for that very reason, because I didn't know how to relax and have fun. That's why I'm here."

A rush of sympathy passed through him. "You're going to be okay, Jorgie," he said. "Everyone gets their heart broken."

"Even you?"

"Well." He chuckled. "I've managed to escape that fate so far, but most everyone else goes through it."

"So you're absolutely no help at all as a shoulder to cry on."

"Maybe not." He wiggled his eyebrows. "But I could provide the comic relief."

"Maybe later," she said, sliding closed the shade over the window portal. "Now if you'll excuse you, I'm going to take a nap."

All righty, then. Quint knew when he'd been summarily dismissed.

THANK HEAVENS she'd gotten rid of him. Relief leaked from Jorgie in a long-held sigh. The last thing she needed right now was her schoolgirl crush going all Casanova on her.

*What do you mean?* She could hear Avery's voice in her head. *That's exactly what you need. A fine fling with someone you know and trust. Why were you being so prickly with him?*

Why? Because the man scared the pants off her. She'd had him tucked away in her mental keepsakes drawer, along with all her other teenage heartthrob fantasies. In her mind he'd been as unobtainable as a rock star and suddenly, poof, he'd been sitting in the seat beside her.

Another troublesome aspect was the fact that thirteen years later, he looked better than ever. And he'd been flirting with her. Quint. The most handsome man she knew. Flirting with her, a woman whose looks were average at best.

*You're only average-looking because you don't make much of an effort. Wear more makeup and jewelry, spend more money on your haircut, and get some sexy clothes.*

"Get out of my head, Avery," she grumbled under her breath. "You took off and left me, now leave."

"Excuse me?" said the flight attendant, leaning over the empty seat beside her that still smelled of Quint's outdoorsy cologne. "Did you need something?"

"No, nothing, thanks." Embarrassed at being caught talking to herself, Jorgie ducked her head.

Okay, clearly she had to make a decision. She and Quint were going to be at the same resort for two weeks. And obviously—although for the life of her, she didn't know why—he seemed attracted to her. So, did she just go with it?

Expand her sexual horizons, fulfill her youthful fantasies, or did she let the past stay buried and keep away from him?

Once upon a time, it would have been a no-brainer. She knew she wasn't Quint's type. He liked fast cars and even faster women. By his own admission, he'd never had his heart broken; by the process of elimination that made him the heartbreaker.

*Unless…*whispered Avery's voice.

Unless what?

*You take full of advantage of him and this vacation. Let him be your love tutor, your rebound guy. That should be right up his alley.*

She had to admit that the idea made perfect sense. It was an excellent solution to her post-Brian doldrums.

## 3

*Movies are made for the voyeurs in us all*
*—Make Love Like a Movie Star*

AVERY BODEL GOT OFF the plane in L.A. feeling freer than she'd felt in, well…forever.

Honestly, she loved Jorgie like a sister, but the girl was so stuck in her ways. Sometimes it was as if she were hanging out with an anchor. She did feel a little badly for having ditched her at the airport the way she did, but it was for Jorgie's own good. It was high time she started having adventures of her own without using Avery as a crutch.

She stood around with the rest of the passengers at the private airstrip, waiting for her baggage to be unloaded from the Eros jet, when she saw him step off the plane. He must have boarded earlier than she had and been sitting in the back of the plane, because she certainly didn't remember ever seeing the guy before and he was not someone you could miss.

If this had been a movie, this would be the point where the director cued the sensual music and brightened the spotlight to focus solely on the devilishly broody-looking man stepping off the plane.

Everything about him was dark. Dark hair, dark eyes, dark look on his face.

Avery's heart thumped. *Dude, now here was a man.*

He wore faded black jeans with a hole in the right knee, a black Nirvana T-shirt that had been washed one too many times. He had on scuffed, scarred military boots and the beard stubble at his jaw declared that he hadn't bothered with a razor in days. Some men might come across as scruffy and unkempt in such attire, but this guy simply sizzled.

Avery felt an instant stirring in her womb. *This one would make a fine baby daddy.* Immediately, she slapped the snooze button on her biological clock.

The last thing she wanted was anything—or anyone— tying her down. You couldn't be footloose with a diaper bag hanging off your shoulder and a kid on your hip. She was only twenty-six. She had a lot more living to do before she settled down. As the oldest of five children, with her baby sister thirteen years younger, she knew all too well how kids consumed your life.

She gave herself a mental shake, but she couldn't stop staring at the guy. He possessed a keep-your-distance aura that made her itch to crowd his personal space. He stepped from her view behind a large man and it was only when she felt her shoulders sag that she realized how tense she'd been.

The attendants set suitcases on the tarmac and everyone gathered around to claim their luggage. Avery and Mr. Broody Loner reached for the same black travel bag at the same time. She got there first, but his hand quickly closed over hers.

His touch was warm and firm and disturbing. Goose bumps spread up her arm.

"That's my bag," he said, his deep, evocative voice under-scoring the authoritative expression on his face. His rugged good looks produced a persona of unadulterated, masculine allure that could turn a vulnerable woman looking for a little excitement into a mindless pile of quivering flesh. Good thing she wasn't the quivery, vulnerable type.

"No." She stood her ground. "No, it's not. That's my bag."

"It's mine," he said. "And I can prove it."

Before she could react, he reached for the zipper and, in one smooth movement, unzipped the bag, just as she yanked on the handle. Immediately, an array of brightly colored thong panties, push-up bras, racy negligees and sex toys spilled out onto the tarmac.

Instantly, his face bloomed red. "Um…um…"

"It's okay to say, 'I'm wrong.'" Avery wrinkled her nose and tossed him a smug smile. If Jorgie were here she'd be mortified. As it was, Avery was having a bit of fun.

His mouth dropped open. "These…" He swept a hand at her sexy lingerie. "This is…"

"Mine," she said firmly, not the least bit embarrassed to have the contents of her naughty drawer strewn around for everyone to see. She wasn't ashamed of her sexuality. "And I do accept your apology, Mr.…."

He laughed then, a rusty noise that sounded as if he didn't use it often. "Stewart," he said. "Jake Stewart."

She stuck out her hand. "Nice to meet you, Jake. I'm Avery, Avery Bodel."

He shook her hand with a steady grip and the sweet zap to her solar plexus turned her inside out. "Sorry about unzipping your bag. I could have sworn it was mine."

"Well, you know you're going to have to make it up to me," she said audaciously. No one had ever accused Avery of being subtle.

"Sure, sure." He went down on one knee, started

plowing through the plethora of panties, bras, teddies, camisoles and bustiers scattered over the ground. Red, black, white, green, purple. Silk, satin, lace. "You got stock in Victoria's Secret?"

"I should, considering all the money I spend in their stores."

"Do you have any regular clothes?"

"They're in my garment bag."

"Ah." Gingerly, he picked up a vibrator, and then he met her gaze with one eyebrow cocked on his forehead.

"Don't judge," she said, and snatched it from him. "A girl doesn't always have access to a fellow who's ready, willing and able." She was charmed to see the tops of his ears burn beet-red. She'd rattled a guy who seemed unshakeable.

"I find that hard to believe."

"Just because a woman can get a guy, it doesn't mean she wants him."

"Does anything embarrass you?" he asked.

"Not much."

"Clearly," he said, stuffing the last of her undergarments back in the bag and zipping it securely shut.

"I've decided how you're going to make it up to me," she said, enjoying this immensely.

He looked uneasy. "How's that?"

"You're taking me out to dinner tonight." And with that parting remark, she gathered up her bags and sashayed away.

JAKE WATCHED HER GO, feeling as if he'd been caught in an avalanche.

Avery Bodel was a force of nature. She was too bold for his tastes. Too bold by half, but there was something about her that was compelling. It was in her sassy walk and her silk-smooth voice. He smelled it in her scent—earthy, spicy, real. He felt it on his skin where she shook his hand. Pure energy, forceful and compelling. And he saw it in the swing of her long dark purple hair and in that sassy little ink art peeking between the top of her low-rise jeans and the hem of her T-shirt.

The sight of that tattoo hardened his cock and startled the hell out of Jake. He hadn't had such a powerful reaction to a woman in a long time. Not since Amanda had left him. Not since before Afghanistan.

At the thought of the war he'd left eighteen months ago, Jake grabbed up his bag filled with camera equipment and followed the rest of the group toward the waiting bus that would take them to the Eros resort nestled in the Hollywood Hills.

Normally, he didn't let himself get distracted from his work, but a woman like her could make any man forget his own name. And he didn't like it. Not one damned bit. He got the feeling she had only one speed and that was balls to the wall. He wondered if she slowed down for anything.

The idea of finding out held far too much appeal. He wasn't about to take her out on a date. Miss Bodel was going to find herself sadly disappointed if she thought she could just say the word and he'd fall right into line. Obviously, she was accustomed to wrapping men around her little finger, but she hadn't counted on Jake Stewart. Nobody told him what to do. Not anymore. Not since he'd left the air force.

*What if she's the saboteur who'd been messing around with Taylor Milton's resorts?*

Jake canted his head, watched her boobs bounce jauntily as she mounted the steps to the bus. His boss, Dougal

Lockhart, had told him to suspect everyone. Guests, employees, even resort security. No one was above suspicion. And Jake was damned good at watching, which was why he liked looking at the world from behind the lens of a camera.

His talent at video photography was the reason why Dougal and Taylor had decided his skills would be best suited to an undercover assignment at the Hollywood resort, making people's voyeuristic fantasies come true at the same time he provided undercover scrutiny for Eros.

Some of the other air marshals at The Lockhart Agency seemed to dislike their undercover assignments; Jake however, found himself enjoying the opportunity to go behind the camera and watch the world from that angle. He learned more from watching people than from conversing with them. Even when he was around others, being behind the camera gave him a sense of aloneness and privacy that he prized. It also allowed him the opportunity to process his feelings and impressions.

Could Avery Bodel be a saboteur? Nah, highly unlikely. She didn't have a poker face. Or a poker body for that matter. He'd seen the flare of sexual interest in her eyes and he certainly noticed the way her nipples beaded under her bra when they'd touched. His instincts told him that with this woman, what you saw was what you got.

Then again, Samson never suspected Delilah and look what happened to him.

Forcing aside thoughts of the spunky Miss Bodel and her luscious body, Jake boarded the bus for the trip to the Eros resort.

He felt an itch to take a camera from the bag and start filming Avery, just so he could figure out what he thought about her. He splayed a palm to the back of his neck. *Stop thinking about her.* He had a job to do and he didn't let anything get in the way of his work. Not even a delicious morsel like Avery.

They arrived at the resort and got checked in. Jake enjoyed seeing the guests' reaction to the over-the-top glitz and glamour of the resort. It put him in mind of an R-rated version of the MGM Grand in Las Vegas. Lavish fountains, sexy movie posters, provocative music piped in through the sound system, clips of erotic scenes being played out on television monitors scattered throughout the resort. As guests checked in, *9 1/2 Weeks* was on.

He walked up to Avery, who was in line for the registration desk. "About that date—"

"Pick me up at eight," she said. "And take a razor to your chin. I'm not a fan of stubble burn."

"Anyone ever tell you that you're bossy as hell?"

"All the time." She batted her lashes.

"Yeah, well, this dog doesn't jump when you snap your fingers. Sorry, I'm otherwise occupied. I can't make the date."

She didn't appear the least bit perturbed. "You're standing me up?"

"I am."

"I can see why you're not married."

"How do you know I'm not married?"

"For one thing, no ring. For another thing, I asked the bus driver."

"You asked about me?"

"Of course. If we're going to be dating, I have to know you're not married. I don't date married men. I got burned once, never again."

"We're not dating."

She simply smiled at him and stepped up to the registration desk as the clerk called, "Next in line."

"We're not," he repeated.

"Uh-huh," she said mildly.

God, but the woman was irritating. He wasn't going to stand here and argue with her. He already had an assigned bungalow. He didn't have to wait in line. Shouldering his bag, he stalked off and he could swear he heard her giggling behind him.

Irritated, he headed for the back exit, wondering what it was about the woman that had gotten under his skin. He didn't like feeling this way. Emotions were messy, troublesome things. He preferred to keep himself above the fray. And now this woman had him squelching emotional impulses right and left.

He let himself into the bungalow decorated to replicate a 1940s era movie set and dumped his bag on the metal table. The table had a green Formica top that reminded him of the one that used to sit in his grandmother's kitchen. Then he took his gun from the holster strapped to his leg and laid it beside the camera bag. He made a quick call to check in with the Lockhart Agency. After that, he moved toward the bathroom. He liked cool showers after a long flight.

But he never made it to the shower. As he passed through the bedroom, he noticed the blinds were open. He moved across the black-and-white tiled floor to draw them closed. Always the watcher, he peeked outside first.

In the bungalow across the way, the blinds were open, as well. The distance between the two dwellings wasn't more than three feet and he could see right inside the other bedroom.

What he saw froze him to the spot with his hand wrapped around the swivel rod of the blinds. His cock hardened, rising up to strain against the zipper of his jeans.

In the bedroom next door, Avery Bodel was stripping off

her clothes right in front of the open window. Her back was to him as she pulled her shirt over her head and gracefully tossed it to the floor. Her hands went to the clasp of her bra, and she slowly undid each eye hook. He could see the ink art on her lower back, a simple dark blue design of tangled vines.

Watching her, his throat convulsed. She slipped off the bra and turned slightly, giving him a side view of her perfect breasts. Not too big, not too small, just the right size. She unsnapped her jeans and shimmied them off, leaving her standing there in nothing but a spectacular red satin thong. His cock throbbed painfully.

He should snap the blinds closed or step away from the window, but he couldn't make himself move. Nothing could wrench his gaze away from the glory of her feminine curves.

She reached up to pull her hair into a ponytail and secure it high on her head with a band. Her complexion was flawless, but he found himself grinning when he spied the cute little dimple in the center of her right butt cheek.

Jake gulped. *Turn away. Turn away.*

But he did not. Could not.

She lifted one long, lean leg up to the corner of the bed, then leaned over to peel off her sock, then repeated the action with her other leg.

His breath was coming in hot, raspy gasps. All the muscles in his body tensed. A groan slipped from his lips and his fingers tightened as he imagined sinking them into the sweet flesh of her rounded bottom and holding on for dear life as he pumped into her.

With her back still to him, she hooked her index finger through the tiny little scrap that constituted her panties and slowly inched the material down, wriggling her hips seductively.

His erection was blinding hard. He couldn't even think, much less breathe. Sweat beaded his forehead from the desire boiling his blood.

Then she turned, head down as she kicked off her panties, giving him a full and unobstructed view of her. Those perfect breasts sported pert pink nipples. A golden ring glinted at her navel. That sweet patch of hair just above her sex told him she was a natural blonde through and through.

She raised her head, stared right into his bedroom window and slyly winked just before she reached out and shuttered the blinds.

# 4

*Initially, withholding affection heightens longing*
*—Make Love Like a Courtesan*

VENICE WAS an architectural symphony. A simmering fantasy of mist and sunshine. A meandering labyrinth of pathways, bridges and canals. A sweet poem of complex dreams.

Jorgie had often daydreamed of visiting the most romantic city on earth. She'd visualized herself strolling the cobblestone streets, gliding the waterways in a graceful gondola, shopping in the popular Rialto district. She imagined she would stop to watch artisans expertly practice the art of blowing glass or mask-making. She'd thirsted to drink Bellinis at a sidewalk café. And she'd thought about kissing Brian on the Bridge of Sighs.

Well, so much for that last part. But she didn't need a man to enjoy Venice. She was young and alive and even though she was scared, she felt a perfect thrill she'd never felt before. It was a delicious combination of curiosity, optimism, hope and excitement. She was on her own in a foreign country and it felt good. Avery had been right. She did need to go it alone for once in her life.

The group arrived via vaporetto, a water taxi sardined

with Eros guests, and by the time they reached the resort, Jorgie was already in love. How had she managed to live twenty-five years without visiting this special place?

The guests were met at the lavish resort—a restored Venetian palace once occupied by royalty—by Eros employees costumed in period clothing from the Italian Renaissance. She found herself searching for Quint in the crowd, but she didn't see him. The bite of disappointment was unexpected. She didn't recall seeing him on the vaporetto, either.

She checked in and turned to go to her room when she spied Quint and her heart went all wonky again.

He was dressed like an eighteenth-century nobleman, in rich fabrics and lush colors of the time. He seemed taller than he'd been on the plane, his eyes sharper, his presence wholly regal. His personality filled the room. His jovial laugh, as he said something to the dozen or so women who collected around him, slid slickly off the thick stone walls.

Here he was, Casanova in the flesh. He glanced over the heads of the other women, caught her gaze and offered a lopsided smile meant only for her.

The other women gaped at him with dumbstruck expressions on their faces, as if the heavens had opened up and he'd come tripping down the stairs just for them. They hung on to his every word. Groupies.

Who knew he had groupies?

Although she longed to join the flock, something inside of Jorgie would not let her puddle at his feet. Yes, he was good-looking. Yes, his smile stirred her soul. Yes, she'd had a crush on him when she was thirteen. Yes, she wanted to kiss him so badly she couldn't breathe, but she sure as heck was not going to let him know that. And be like all the others? No way. She had her pride.

She turned, headed toward the exit.

"Jorgie," he called.

Well, she couldn't very well ignore him now, could she? That would be rude. She stopped, turned back. "Quint, oh, hi, I didn't see you there," she lied nonchalantly.

"Excuse me, ladies." He threw a smile and a wink to the women. Jorgie thought they were going to melt on the spot. "I need to speak to an old friend."

He covered the distance between them, linked his arm through hers and pulled her into the corridor. "Thanks, shrimp."

"Shrimp?" She arched an eyebrow.

"It's what Keith and I used to call you."

"I can't believe you remembered that," she said, feeling way more flattered than she should. He'd called her shrimp as a big brotherly term of affection. That meant he saw her as a little sister or an old friend, not a potential sex partner.

"Well…" He raked his gaze over her. "I shouldn't use the nickname on you. It's shrimp no more. You're all grown up."

"So what were you thanking me for?" she asked, glossing right over that comment.

He punched the button for the elevator. "Rescuing me from my adoring public."

Jorgie snorted. "Hey, you can't handle the adoration, don't dress up like Casanova."

"You have no idea what a huge burden it is," he teased, and struck a preening pose. "Being such a sexy beast."

Jorgie rolled her eyes. "Poor you."

"You're pitiless."

"I don't have much tolerance for nonsense—"

He nodded. "You're good for me," he said. "I need

someone to call my bluff. I gotta admit, playing Casanova messes with your head."

"Don't blame Casanova. You were like that in high school and I have a feeling you've been like that ever since."

He looked into her eyes. "What can I say? There's nothing that makes life worth living like having a beautiful woman at your side. What room are you in?" he asked as the elevator opened and he got on with her.

She should have told him it was none of his business, but damn if that endearing grin of his didn't slip past her defenses. "214."

"The blue room." He punched the elevator button for the second floor. "Lady Pompadour stayed there. Did you know she and Casanova were lovers?"

"Good for them."

"You're really hard to impress, you know that?"

"It's all the number crunching. Tends to give one a 'bottom line' approach to life."

Quint stepped back and stared boldly at her bottom.

"Mason," she said sharply, using his last name to indicate she was displeased with his frisky behavior, but a small part of her was thrilled. It was the same part of her that had been secretly relieved when Brian had left.

*"Gerard."* The elevator settled on the second floor with a ping and they got off together.

"You're mocking me."

He lowered his eyelids and slanted a sexy look her way. "It's hard not to. You look so serious."

"Here we are," she said. "214. You've escorted me to my room, you can go now." She slashed her key card through the computerized reader installed in the door handle and kneed the door open.

"Wait." He touched her forearm.

Instantly, the hairs on her arms lifted. He said nothing for a moment. His gaze hooked on her. She forced herself to hold his stare. "Yes?" she whispered.

"Sit with me at dinner."

"Why?"

"Fend off the she-wolves."

"Don't give me that. You love the she-wolves."

"Okay, here's the deal. You remind me of home. I don't see my folks much. Gordy's married with kids. I just wanted someone to talk to about old times." He sounded so sincere.

But Jorgie didn't trust it. She narrowed her eyes. "This isn't some Casanova ploy to get me into bed, is it?"

"I'm shocked that you would suggest such a thing." He feigned innocence. "Is it working?"

*Yes.* "No."

"Come on," he cajoled, his gaze caressing her face. "For old times' sake?"

A shiver of awareness tripped down Jorgie's spine, dueling madly with the part of her that wanted to invite him to join her in bed. She knew he was a playboy. It was clear he'd been well cast as Casanova, but she couldn't stop the gut-level reaction that whispered "Go for it" into her ear.

The problem was that pesky high school crush. If he was just a good-looking guy interested in a good time, she might be willing go for it. He could very easily be her first casual fling. But there was that nagging infatuation that had had her doodling in her notebook, *Mrs. Jorgie Mason*, when she was thirteen.

She had two fears about that. One, what if she did have a fling with Quint and it turned out to be lousy? The sweet fantasy of him would be lost to her forever. Then there was the very real possibility that sex with him would be dynamic, unlike anything she'd ever experienced, and she'd fall in love with him all over again, while he blithely went on his merry way. She wasn't in any emotional condition to deal with that.

"Pretty please?" He flashed her one of his trademark smiles and for a fraction of a second that devilish come-play-with-me grin had her on the edge of throwing caution to the wind. Then she thought about how he'd given her that same smile when he was sixteen just before he pulled a prank on her.

Still…he was right. They would both be eating dinner in the main dining hall with the tour group. Why not sit at his table? He had once been her brother's best friend. It would be rude, wouldn't it, to deny his request? Plus, they'd be in a public place. What could happen? Maybe he could even teach her a few tricks about how to have an affair while keeping her heart out of the fray of emotional involvement.

"All right," she conceded, wondering what she was thinking. The cold shoulder she'd given him on the plane was really the only way to deal with a footloose guy like Quint, especially when she was feeling so vulnerable.

"See you at eight." He winked and strolled out the door.

Jorgie stared after him, awash in the wake of his sexy aura. What in the devil had she just opened herself up for? She'd gotten what she'd come on this trip for. A date with a sexy man to help her forget about what had happened with Brian. But she hadn't expected that man to be the same guy who'd once dominated her girlhood fantasies. A guy who made her feel both shivery and sweaty at the same time.

*He's not really interested in you,* she reminded herself. *It's just the challenge. As long as you don't get caught up in his charm, you'll be fine. This is your chance for a true, no-strings sexual adventure. Grab it with both hands and hang on for dear life.*

AN HOUR LATER, Quint was sitting in a plush leather chair in an equally plush office that made him antsy. He'd been summoned here by Taylor Milton herself, who'd just flown in on her private jet, and he couldn't help wondering what he'd done wrong.

Taylor was thirty-four and looked exactly like what she was, an airline heiress. Five foot six, redheaded and sharp-eyed, a lithe package of ballerina grace and bulldog tenacity that had shot her to the top of an industry that had fallen on hard times. She'd taken her father's plain vanilla commuter airline and turned it into the only adult-oriented airline/destination resort in the world. Quint had also noticed she was fair, but demanding. She wanted what she wanted when she wanted it. Nor was she a woman easily swayed by an easy grin. On that score, she reminded him of Jorgie.

As he sat there, his anxiety growing, his boss, Dougal Lockhart, walked through the door.

Uh-oh. The shit must have hit the fan if they were tag-teaming him. Quickly, he ran through his mind, trying to think how his behavior might have caused this meeting. The morality clause he'd signed for Eros forbade him from having sex with the guests, but it didn't say a word about fellow employees. On his last tour here, he and Gwen, the woman who'd played the part of his Casanova conquest, had had a very good time together. Was that what this was about? He was enjoying his work too much?

Dougal stalked over and perched on the corner of Taylor's desk.

"What's up?" Quint asked, flashing his ready smile to abate his anxiety.

"Taylor's received another threatening letter," Dougal began. "And we've determined it was written on a computer at this resort. Unfortunately, it was from a computer in the Internet café, so anyone could have sent it."

"There's a log-in record," Quint pointed out.

"Yes, but if the person leaves without signing out anyone can take their place and still be logged in under their name," Taylor explained. "In fact, we suspect the perpetrator haunted the Internet café just waiting for someone who forgot to log out."

Quint was getting the feeling someone had sent the e-mail under his name. He wracked his brain trying to think of the last time he'd used the Internet café. "So who did you trace it back to?"

"Gwen Kemp," Dougal said.

"You think Gwen is in on the sabotage?"

Taylor shifted in her seat, picked up a pencil and drummed it against the top of her desk. "We don't believe so. Dougal grilled her for over an hour and she does have airtight alibis for most of the sabotage incidents that have occured at the resorts over the course of the last several months."

"I'm sensing a 'but' here," Quint said.

"But," Dougal supplied, "we can't take any chances, so Gwen has been suspended until we can determine who sent the e-mail under her address."

"You might never find out."

"We'll find out," Dougal said firmly. "This crap stops now."

"I agree. You got a copy of the e-mail?"

Dougal pulled a folded piece of paper from his pocket

and passed it to Quint. He unfolded it and read the vitriolic message.

> No more pussyfooting around, Princess, this is it. You're going down in a big way. After I get through with you, you'll be standing in line for food stamps. You think those air marshals you hired as security for your planes and resorts can protect you? They haven't done much good so far, have they? I'll hit when and where you least expect it. Nothing can stop me. Ciao for now.

"This is personal," Quint said.

Dougal nodded solemnly. "We need to be hypervigilant."

"Of course."

"There's also the matter of Gwen's replacement," Taylor said. "We don't have time to hire and train another actress to play the part of your love conquest for the Casanova course."

"You're ditching the class." Quint sat up straighter in his chair.

"No," Taylor said. "We have thirty-seven men signed up for your course. Enrollment has skyrocketed since you took over the class, Quint."

"I told you he was a natural-born charmer," Dougal said.

"He's hot," Taylor agreed. "You have that nice blend of boyish charm and manly audacity that women thrive on. If you weren't working for Dougal, I'd hire you in a heartbeat."

Quint felt a twin surge of pride and embarrassment. Truth was, he enjoyed playing Casanova, but he was also a bit sheepish about it. He shrugged. "Aw, shucks, ma'am, it's nothing."

"See, right there." Taylor pointed. "That's what I'm

talking about. You know you're handsome but you have a way about you that says you don't take it too seriously."

"Life's too short to take it seriously."

"Exactly."

"So if you're not replacing Gwen with a new actress and you're not canceling the course, who is Casanova going to demonstrate his seduction techniques on?"

"Me," Taylor said.

Quint gulped. The woman scared him. "You?"

"I'm very happily married," Taylor said. "I'm immune to your charms."

"Maybe," Quint protested, "but Casanova's romance is going to look like the put-up job it is if anyone recognizes you."

"Do you have a better idea?" Dougal asked.

He thought of Jorgie. "As a matter of fact, I do."

Taylor leaned back in her chair. "I'm all ears."

"An old friend of mine just happens to be staying at the resort," Quint said. "I've known her since we were teenagers. We're just friends, it's never been anything more, and she's here nursing a broken heart. I think she'd be the perfect person to play Casanova's conquest."

"Hmm." Taylor studied him pensively. "It's a thought."

"Do you think she'll do it?" Dougal asked.

"I'm having dinner with her tonight. I'll ask," he said, searching for anything to keep from having to try out Casanova's power of seduction on Taylor.

"I don't know," Taylor mused. "This could cause you some trouble in your relationship with her."

"Don't worry," Quint said. "I see her as nothing more than a kid sister."

"Well, then." Taylor beamed. "We settled that easier than I thought."

Dougal called the head of resort security, Frank Lavoy, a barrel-chested man in his mid-forties who'd worked under Dougal in the air force, into the office for the rest of the meeting. Dougal launched into the heightened security protocol he was instituting at the resorts and his expectations from Quint and Frank.

Quint listened, nodded, absorbed the information, but in the back of his mind, his thoughts were on Jorgie. He could see one major flaw in his plan.

One huge obstacle loomed. He'd flat-out lied to Taylor. He had the hots for the woman who'd once been the pig-tailed sister of his best friend. He hadn't counted on getting an opportunity to practice Casanova's seduction techniques on her and he found himself wondering just how far he could push the envelope.

Just then, a knock sounded on the door.

"Come in," Taylor called out.

The door opened and an older, heavyset man with gray hair stepped over the threshold, a well-dressed woman in her early sixties by his side. "Hey there, princess," he said.

"Chuck, Mitzi." Taylor's face dissolved into a welcoming grin. She hopped from behind the desk and went to hug the couple. "What are you doing here?"

"We were in Rome," Mitzi said, "and Chuck remembered it was your birthday so we called your office and your sweet little secretary told us you were here, so of course we had to come to Venice. We haven't seen you since your wedding! How's Daniel?"

"Fabulous," Taylor said, referring to her new husband.

"We're taking you out to dinner," Chuck announced.

"Dougal, Quint." Taylor gestured. "This is General Charles Miller and his wife, Mitzi. Dear friends of the family."

Quint and Dougal shook first General Miller's hand and then his wife's.

"Chuck and Mitzi are my godparents. They're the aunt and uncle I never had," Taylor explained.

"Any leads on who could be making those threats?" Mitzi asked.

Taylor sighed. "Not so far."

General Miller glowered. "Have you considered changing the direction of your resorts?"

"Meaning what?" Taylor asked.

The general shrugged. "Perhaps this person or persons would back off if your resorts weren't so…" He paused and Quint could tell he was choosing his words carefully. "Controversial."

Taylor sank her hands on her hips. "Are you suggesting I allow someone to threaten me into abandoning the business model that's made me so successful?"

"It might have made you successful—" Miller stiffened and his eyes narrowed "—but it's also made you a target. If your father was alive—"

"My father would be amazed that I've tripled the net worth of his airline in six short years," Taylor interrupted. "I know you don't approve of the concept of Eros resorts, Chuck, but I believe I provide a much-needed service, which my profits bear out."

"My," Mitzi said in a loud voice, clearly trying to change the hot topic of conversation, and cast her gaze over Quint. "Don't you look dashing."

"He's Casanova," Taylor said.

General Miller's face darkened. "The famous libertine."

He sounded so gruff, Quint rushed to point out, "It's just a costume. Some fun role-playing for the guests."

The general frowned, reminding Quint why he left the air force. Too much rank and discipline for his tastes.

"Well, I don't know about you, Taylor," Mitzi said, intervening again, "but I'm starving." She looked at her husband. "I made reservations for six-thirty and it's after six. Maybe we should be going."

"I'm ready." Taylor linked her arm through the general's and she and Mitzi escorted him out.

# 5

*When in doubt, do the unexpected*
*—Make Love Like a Courtesan*

AT SEVEN-THIRTY, Jorgie put the finishing touches on her makeup in the bathroom of her courtesan-inspired suite and then walked into the lavish sitting area done up in rich fabrics, heavy furniture and lushly detailed tapestries. She could see how courtesans had thrived in such sensual surrounds. The thick textures compelled the fingertips. Velvet cushions stretched over smooth, hard mahogany chairs. Intricately woven brocade pillows. Shimmering golden threads sewn through burgundy damask.

But the sensory appeal of the room did not stop with the tactile.

The room smelled of love, as well. Real flowers adorned numerous vases—roses and stargazer lilies and baby's breath scented the room with the sweet aroma of courtship. Their tender buds were like secret sex organs, releasing their aromatic juices into the air.

Heady stuff.

Jorgie, feeling unnerved and overwhelmed, retrieved her cell phone from her purse and then sank down on the couch that hugged her in an opulent embrace and called Avery.

Her friend answered. "Hello?"

"Hey, you," Jorgie said.

"What's up?" She yawned again.

Jorgie pushed a strand of errant hair back off her forehead. "I've got a date."

"Already?" Her tone changed a little. She could hear Avery's grin. "Wow, I should have abandoned you to your own devices a long time ago. So tell me about the lucky guy?"

She hesitated, not sure she wanted to be completely honest with Avery. She worried she'd tease and she didn't want to be teased about Quint.

"Well?" Avery prodded. "You did call me."

Jorgie cleared her throat. "It's Quint Mason."

"Oooh, the plot thickens."

An emotion she couldn't name tap-danced around in her head. Jorgie bit down on her index finger. "I'm scared."

"What about?"

"I like him."

"And?"

"That's just it. I like him."

"Why does that frighten you?"

"Because I know what kind of man he is and I know what kind of woman I am and, well…we don't match."

"Hey, this isn't supposed to be a forever kind of love. This vacation is all about exploring your sexual horizons, and who better to do that with than a man you know and trust, a man who's not going to get his heart broken when you kiss and part ways at the end of the trip. He's perfect."

She thought about having sex with Quint. The image popped too readily into her mind. His hard body pressed against her soft one. "I know, and that's what scares me. I don't know if I can have a casual fling. What if I'm just not built that way?"

"Then don't have sex with him."

Alarm snapped through her, quick like whiplash. "But I want to have sex with him."

"Then have sex with him."

"I don't want to end up getting hurt."

Avery sighed. "You think too much. Just go with the flow. Let it be. Let whatever happens be okay. Insert your carefree adage here. You can do this."

How very Zen. Maybe if she thought about numbers that would help. Numbers calmed her. They were rational, expected, no surprise with numbers. No emotions, either. She took a deep breath. "Thanks for talking me down."

"No problem."

"So how are things in L.A.?"

"Hmm," Avery said, "they're a bit frustrating."

"How so?"

"I spied a guy I was interested in on the plane. In fact, he's a cameraman for Eros. I asked him out for dinner, but he told me he wasn't interested."

"And you took no for an answer?"

"Well, for now."

"He won't know what hit him." Jorgie chuckled. "I'll let you go. Be safe."

"You, too."

She'd just switched off her phone when a knock sounded on her door. She went to peer out the peephole and her stomach did a slow slide to her shoes.

Quint. Looking exceedingly handsome in a suit and tie. How come he was picking her up? They were just supposed to meet in the dining hall. And why was he wearing a suit. Feeling self-conscious that she hadn't dressed up enough, Jorgie ran a hand over the front of her simple cotton dress, dithering about whether to go change or not.

He knocked again.

*Don't just stand there with your mouth open,* Avery's voice said inside her head. *Let the man in.*

Taking a deep breath to steady her jangled nerves, she opened the door. Quint met her with a grin and his patented come-hither gaze, his dark hair combed back off his forehead. He smelled of soap and crisp green apples.

The minute he saw her, his eyes flashed like hot licorice. He raked his eyes over her dress. "Wow, you look great in green."

"Is it okay? I didn't realize dinner was so dressy, I mean you're in a suit and—"

"You're perfect," he said, and extended his elbow to her. "Ready to go down to dinner?"

"Um…yes, you didn't have to come fetch me, you know."

"I know," he said warmly.

They went downstairs to the elegant dining room. The buffet spread out before them was a feast for an entire kingdom—prime rib and roasted chicken and braised pork tenderloin. Vegetables of every variety served as delicious side dishes—purple eggplant in a coating of parmesan cheese, sautéed red and green bell peppers, tomatoes with buffalo mozzarella, garlic mashed potatoes, baked yams, broad beans swimming in butter, and crunchy salad greens. There was rye bread and pumpernickel and thick yeasty loaves of French bread.

Jorgie loaded up her plate and followed Quint to a small bistro table for two. Most of the other guests were sitting at the long communal table. "We can sit over there with everyone else," she said.

"I'd like to sit here." He set down his plate, and then turned to pull out the chair for her. "A little privacy would be nice."

Oh, wow. Blowing out her breath, she sat and he took his seat across from her.

"There's something I want to ask you," he said as she spread her napkin in her lap.

"Uh-huh."

"The request is a bit unorthodox."

Was she really ready to get personal and private with him? Jorgie picked up the steak knife and held it with her thumb against the back of the blade. "What's up?"

"I don't really know how to broach the subject, so I'm just going to come right out and ask it."

"Okay."

"Here's the deal." Quint spread his hands out on the table. "I need you to be my plant."

"Excuse me? Your what?"

"Plant."

"As in a Benjamin Ficus, ponytail palm, English ivy?"

He laughed. "No, as in someone in a talk show audience who plays off the riffs of the host."

She frowned. "I'm still not sure what you're asking of me."

He threaded a hand through his hair. "I'm not explaining this very well. As an instructor for How To Make Love Like Casanova, I'm expected to show results."

"Ookay."

"I have to get a woman to fall in love with me."

"That shouldn't be very hard for you to do," she said, ignoring the weird churning in her stomach and the sudden quickening in the pace of her heartbeat.

"But it would be cruel to just pick someone at random and work Casanova's charms on her and then just drop her. Plus, there is that morality clause in my contract with Eros," he mused.

"It would be cruel," she agreed.

"Which is why Eros hires actors to mingle among the guests. It's for the instructors to demonstrate their seduction techniques on."

"Gotcha."

"My plant quit today," Quint said. "But by the time we get someone else hired and trained this tour will be half over. So I was wondering, since we're friends, if you'd be my plant."

Her feelings took a hit. Like they had in college when a really cute guy she'd been mooning over asked her out and then in the middle of the meal tried to hire her to do his calculus homework. Same deal here. Same sour-stomach sensation.

Quint had asked her to be his plant because he knew she was someone he couldn't fall in love with. She didn't know why that bothered her. The man was a drop-dead gorgeous ten and she was a five-and-a-half at best, maybe a six with makeup and the right hair style. But Jorgie kind of liked the little hump on the bridge of her nose.

Maybe that was a mistake, liking her imperfections. Her body wasn't bad, a size twelve, although she was a little curvier than most of her friends. Nice. She looked nice. Friendly, approachable, but dull as paste.

"You mean you need someone you know you won't fall in love with," she said.

"Exactly." He looked too pleased.

She scowled. "While you want *me* to fall madly in love with you."

"Yeah, you know, but not for real, of course, just for show."

"No worries there," she said half perkily, half sarcastically, both belying what she was really feeling. Clearly, he wasn't attracted to her the way she was attracted to him. Why should she be surprised by that? "What do I get out of the deal?"

"I talked to my boss about it. Your trip will be comped."

Well, that was a deal. An Eros vacation did not come cheap. Jorgie raised a hand. "So let me get this straight. You want me to pretend to fall in love with you, in a public way, in front of the guys you're teaching pick-up artist techniques to, and for that I get a free vacation?"

"That's it." He grinned.

Good thing she was sitting down because her knees suddenly went swimming, warm and weak like melted butter.

"But," he said, "I don't want you to make it easy for me."

She cocked her head. "No? Why not?"

"Can't let it look rigged."

"It is rigged."

"Yeah, but we want to maintain the fantasy. Besides, Casanova loves a challenge."

"Are we talking about Casanova here, or you?"

"Hey, all guys love the thrill of the chase. It's in our nature."

"Okay, so what do you want me to do?"

"Act like I just said something repugnant. Jump to your feet, knock over your chair. Call me names, slap me across the face."

Jorgie narrowed her eyes. "Are you into some kind of secret masochistic kink?"

"No, it's part of the show."

The thought of doing what he asked and drawing undue attention to herself made Jorgie's stomach contract. "I still think it sounds kinky."

"I didn't say smack me hard. Just make a scene."

"I'm not… This doesn't…"

"You're embarrassed."

"Yeah, well, sort of."

What he did next took her completely by surprise. One minute he was grinning at her impishly, the next minute he was full-on kissing her.

Shock shot through her. Not from his kiss, but from how damn quickly it aroused her. Startled, she jumped to her feet.

"That's it," he goaded. "Let me have it for boorishly manhandling you."

If he wanted her to play the role of his hard-to-get lover, then by gosh, she was playing hard to get. "How dare you," she yelled.

"Good, good."

Heads turned. Conversations ground to a dead halt and the fact that they were looking at her caused Jorgie's cheeks to burn.

"I've never been so insulted in my life!" When with that pronouncement, she slapped him lightly across the face, and knocked over a chair as she stormed away.

The room fell dead silent.

Now she knew what it felt like to be a woodland creature crossing the road in the middle of the night just as a sports car zoomed around the corner.

Roadkill.

TWO HOURS LATER, Jorgie lay in bed staring at the ceiling, her entire body tingling. She didn't want to think about the kiss Quint had given her. She knew it was all for show. But she couldn't seem to think about anything else.

How brief it had been. A second only. Two at the most and yet… Whew.

She'd wanted more. So much damned more it freaked her out.

*It's the unexpectedness of it. That's all.* There was nothing inherently terrific about his kiss.

*Oh, you are such a liar.*

She touched her nose to see if it was growing. Okay, fine. It had been so fine she'd stopped breathing. And what she'd secretly wanted, wished for, was for him to press harder, take the kiss deeper.

But not there in front of everyone, of course. Then again, if they'd been someplace private, no telling how far he might have taken things.

She blushed in the darkness, embarrassed both by her unexpected need and the silly theatrics she'd performed in the dining hall.

*You need some fun. Take Avery's advice. Let whatever happens be okay.*

That was difficult to do because while he'd kissed her, she'd known it was all for show. He hadn't meant anything by it. He'd chosen to kiss her because she was safe. A pal, a friend, a buddy to play his plant. Someone he knew he couldn't fall for.

She clenched the sheets in her fists and let out a noise of frustration. Why had she agreed to this?

Free vacation.

Oh, yeah. But in retrospect, was it really worth it? Gnawing her bottom lip, she flipped over onto her side. Sleep, sleep, go to sleep.

She couldn't stop remembering, though, how it had felt to have Quint's firm lips pressed against hers—tantalizing, exciting, awe inspiring.

*He didn't mean it. Stop fantasizing about him. It wasn't that good of a kiss.*

No, no, but it could have been.

Sleep, sleep.

Okay, she'd try.

After she'd fled the dining room, she'd heard murmurs in her wake.

*"Who's that girl who slapped Casanova?"*

*"She turned him down and she looks like that?"*

*"What was she thinking? There's tons of pretty girls here."*

*"I'm prettier. I'm gonna go give him the key to my room. The man should not have to spend the night alone."*

*"You better hurry up, Hannah's over there talking to him and unless I'm mistaken, she just handed him her panties."*

Hmph. She'd had no reason to feel embarrassed in front of those people. They should feel embarrassed for judging her based on her looks and for being so ready to move in on Quint.

*Now* you're *judging* them. *He's free game.* Handsome and single and playing the field. Let them be his plant. She didn't need this. Free vacation be damned.

She flopped onto her back again. This was a bad idea. She should simply tell Quint the deal was off. She didn't want to be his fake conquest.

Ah, who was she kidding? She was jealous, and she'd never looked good in green.

# 6

*The mind is the ultimate aphrodisiac*
*—Make Love Like Casanova*

"GIACOMO CASANOVA was born right here in Venice in 1725," Quint told the group of men gathered for his class.

Most of his students were single, nerdy-looking, socially awkward types who basically lacked self-esteem when it came to approaching women. Quint was quite confident that if they took his advice they'd soon be on their way to exciting love lives, and he'd told them so. They'd sat up straighter just hearing that. Now they waited, eyes on him, poised to take notes.

He felt a powerful thrill in teaching that he hadn't expected. He loved being an air marshal—the travel, the women, the freedom—but teaching filled a space in him that he hadn't known was empty. It gave him a worthwhile feeling. Being an air marshal was all about looking for the bad things in people. It was the nature of a teacher to find and nurture the good.

And Quint liked looking on the bright side, but no matter how much he was enjoying this little avocation, he could not forget the real reason he was here. To protect Taylor Milton's interest. He gazed at his class roster and noticed the red stars beside a few of the names, indicating they'd taken the class before under the regular instructor, who'd been given a paid sabbatical while Quint assumed the faculty role. He'd keep an extra-close eye on those students.

"Casanova was the son of actors, which back then was not a noble profession. Actresses usually doubled as prostitutes and actors were often their pimps. So as you can imagine, the young boy was introduced to the realities of sexual behavior at a tender age."

Some of the students scribbled in notepads, others typed into compact computers.

"His parents traveled around plying their trades, and he felt shame about his mother's reputation. But what hurt him more was her abandonment. Her love was conditional. It came and went. He wrote in his memoirs about being sent away to Padua, where he received a formal education, but he was still bitter and angry about being separated from his mother," Quint continued.

"You expect us to buy that Casanova's sexy behavior was all the fault of his parents?" asked one cocky guy at the back of the room. In every class there was always one. The smart-ass, the rebel who challenged everything Quint had to impart. He realized that Joe Vincent was one of those who'd taken the class last winter about the same time Taylor's Venetian resort was the first to experience sabotage.

"Not at all, Joe," Quint said mildly. "I'm just giving you a bit of background on what molded Casanova."

"So what about you?" Joe asked. "How come you're not married?"

"We're not talking about me."

"You're playing the part of Casanova," Joe challenged. "You have a colorful past with the ladies, from what I hear. What motivates you? Did your mommy not love you enough?"

The rest of the students snickered and glanced from Joe to Quint and back again. He had to take back control of the class or things could turn ugly quick. This was the one thing that made teaching a trial—students who questioned your authority. Still, he supposed it was good for an instructor to reevaluate his methods occasionally.

"Let's just say I haven't found the right woman yet."

"So you're not like Casanova, constantly in pursuit of that which you can never catch?"

"No," Quint denied. Was he? The question blindsided him, but he pushed it aside and trudged on. To his relief, Joe shut up. "Casanova was a complicated guy. He received a doctor-of-law degree in Padua," he said, "proving his lifelong contention that the mind is the ultimate aphrodisiac. He used his facileness with words, among other tools and techniques, to seduce women, and that's what we're going to be learning over the course of these next two weeks. I'm also going to choose a woman from the guests at the resort as my conquest, so you can see Casanova's techniques in action."

"You're going to seduce someone as a demonstration?" said a thin guy in his early twenties with thick-framed glasses and mussed-up hair. "Sweet."

Quint thought about Jorgie. After she'd slapped his face and stalked from the dining hall, he'd felt a surge of attraction so strong he'd had to stay seated until his erection abated. Now, he could hardly wait to see her again and put his Casanova techniques into action. He was ready to prove they worked. Just thinking about her, his hand strayed to the cheek she'd slapped and he grinned. She was feisty. How come he'd never noticed that about her before?

"Maybe that's why you haven't found the right woman," Joe threw in. "You're too busy treating them like sex objects."

"Seriously, dude, what's your problem?" one of the other students chimed in. "We *want* to know how to treat women like sex objects. It's why we're here."

Was it? That bothered Quint. He didn't treat women like sex objects. When he was with a woman, he was with her. He didn't cheat. He didn't lie.

*Yeah, but you've never been with anyone longer than four months.* That was because after the four-month mark, a woman started expecting a commitment.

"Casanova was a risk-taker," he went on, in spite of feeling suddenly conflicted about what he was doing. "He loved intrigue and persuaded high-born noblewomen to make love with him in all kinds of dicey places—inside a speeding carriage, in a closet while the woman's snoring husband slept in the bed, at a public execution. He was young, good-looking, well educated and inventive. He enjoyed the company of older women, as well. When it came to the fairer sex, Casanova was not choosy. He loved them all. He was a rake, a scoundrel. No wall was too high, no gate too barbed to keep him out. When he wanted a woman, he went after her with every weapon in his arsenal. And he was always genuinely in love with the woman he was pursuing and his passion for her was irresistible to the woman. But once they fell in love with him, he left her, just like his mother had left him."

Quint paused in his monologue and looked out at the students. He had them so spellbound they'd stopped taking notes and were just listening, hanging on his every word, imagining that they themselves were Casanova the libertine. He loved holding them in his thrall. Even the tough case, Joe, was leaning forward, ears pricked.

Lowering his voice for dramatic effect, Quint continued. "But there was one woman for whom he burned truly, deeply, and she drew him like a magnet. She was Lady Evangeline, reported to be the illegitimate daughter of Louis the fifteenth and one of his courtesans. Evangeline was the most beautiful woman at court. Every man who saw her desired her. But Lady Evangeline was a tease. She led Casanova on a merry chase without giving in, alternately tantalizing him with seductive smiles and dismissing him with haughty snubs. She drained him of his money and power, and made mincemeat of his heart. She defused him, rendered him useless, and yet he kept coming back for more. He pined for her all his life but they never fully consummated their explosive affair."

"Vicious cock tease," Joe said.

Several other students murmured in agreement.

"Okay, then." Quint pressed his palms together in a single clap. "That concludes the history of Casanova. Now, we're going to move on to some of the techniques he used to seduce his conquests. Tip number one. Appreciate her for her mind, no matter how great her tits are."

The guy in the glasses raised his hand.

"Yes, Spencer?" Quint asked.

"Um, exactly how do you do that?"

"Look her in the eyes, not in the tits. You'll have plenty of time once you win her over to get to those juicy breasts. And listen really listen, to what she has to say."

"Aw, man," someone else said. "Girl talk is so boring."

"Oh, no, that's where you're wrong." Quint shook a finger at the guy. "Girl talk is the key to the kingdom, and once you know how to use it to your advantage, the palace is yours."

"So you're going to show us how this works, right?" Spencer asked.

"Yes." He nodded. "Tonight. On our gondola tour of the city."

"LADY EVANGELINE was one of the most sought-after courtesans in the Venetian court," said Maggie Cantrell, the woman teaching the Make Love like A Courtesan course. She was as diminutive as a munchkin, pushing sixty with a strong tail wind, and she spoke in a slow, measured, deep-throated voice. "Men wrote poetry about her. Women wanted to be her. Children adored her. Evangeline's beauty was legendary."

Maggie clicked the button to advance her PowerPoint presentation and the image of a young woman dressed in the regalia of the Venetian court in the mid-eighteenth century filled the screen. "But as you can see, in actuality, she was not an exceptional beauty. She was, in fact, rather ordinary. But because she was so adept at the art of seduction, people saw her as a rare beauty, even though she was not."

Hmm. Jorgie leaned forward, eyes narrowed, to study the on-screen image of Lady Evangeline.

"Her number one rule for bringing men to their knees was always pay less attention to your admirer than he pays to you. For every three times you feel him looking at you, glance at him once. However, if you want the strongest seductive power over him, when your eyes do meet, do not be the first one to look away."

Jorgie jotted down this piece of advice, feeling she was getting the eighteenth-century version of *The Rules,* although it appeared the advice on seducing a man hadn't changed much in three centuries.

"Remember," Maggie said, "this was her advice on

getting a man to fall in lust with you, not love. Love is a horse of a different color and involves more than just sexy mind games. The tragedy of Lady Evangeline was that she could not let herself have the one man she truly loved, Giacomo Casanova. She knew if she ever gave herself to him fully, she would lose the libertine. As it was, they burned for each other, but their psychology kept them apart. So, in short, if you're looking for true love, find advice from someone other than Lady Evangeline. But if you're looking to seduce, well, you can't go wrong following her techniques."

The women in the room tittered, discussing love versus seduction and how difficult it was to separate one from the other. Jorgie listened with one ear while her mind strayed to thoughts of Quint. Would Lady Evangeline's advice work on him? Could she get him to fall in lust with her?

She thought of Brian and what he'd said about her being lousy in bed, not having a romantic soul. His exact words? "You've got a calculator where your sexuality should be." He'd said that after she'd told him that she wasn't buying a three-hundred-dollar French maid's costume to spice up their sex life.

Brian was right, she realized with a painful start. She did not have a romantic soul. That was why she was here. More than anything she wanted to learn how to seduce a man with one of Lady Evangeline's come-hither looks. She wanted men to think she was beautiful even when she wasn't. She was going to claim her sexual power, and playing Lady Evangeline to Quint's Casanova was the key.

"Don't be afraid to ignore your target," Maggie went on. "Cancel a date. Stand him up. But only if you know he is already interested in you. Doing this will add intrigue to his interest. He'll start wondering why you're ignoring him and who you're with when you're not with him."

The more Maggie talked, the more excited Jorgie became at the prospect of seducing Quint. She didn't know why, but the idea of bringing the man to his knees sent a thrill jolting right through her.

"Seduction," Maggie said, "is all about who has the power. Claim your power now."

Several of the women in the class cheered.

"Tonight, we have a flotilla of gondolas lined up to take us on an evening tour of the city. After dinner, we'll all meet outside the palace. This will be your prime opportunity to practice the skills you've learned today. Dress sexily, show a little skin, but remember, men often feel guilty for objectifying a woman. Evangeline had much more to give than just her body. She had a razor-sharp wit and a keen mind. She could converse on art and music and literature. For now, I want you to go back to your rooms and practice in front of a mirror sending a seductive look, and then I want you to spend time in the hotel museum and art gallery, familiarizing yourself with the lore and allure of the eighteenth century. Class dismissed."

Heart thumping with excitement, Jorgie stood up and followed her classmates out into the hallway, just as Quint's classroom let out across the corridor. Men and women converged in a cauldron of inflamed testosterone and estrogen. The smell of sex wafted off the walls of the old stone building.

She spied Quint in the crowd, a head taller than most of the men. He caught her gaze. She held it, refusing to look away. *I'm Lady Evangeline.*

He kept staring.

She did not blink. *I won't be the first to look away.*

She inhaled deeply into the heady scent of the moment. She could almost touch the pheromone-rich air vibrating between them. Her nose detected all the subtle molecules bursting—frankincense, sandalwood, sage, oak moss, nutmeg, cedarwood, black pepper. It was so thick and clear she suspected that Eros had intentionally seeded the air with earthy aromas.

His gaze wavered, the smile that had started up his lips never formed. His pupils narrowed, his forehead wrinkled in a quizzical expression. She wanted so badly to look away. Staring at him was much too intense and she wasn't the type of person who confronted things head-on. This felt like aggression and it made her uncomfortable. Maybe she just wasn't cut out to be a seductress.

And then Quint lowered his eyelids. He was the first to break their gaze.

She'd won!

She barely had time to revel in the conquest when he was back, looking at her with the narrowed eyes of a predator.

Yipes!

This time, she would have looked away except a man even taller than Quint passed between them, breaking their eye contact. She took the opportunity to escape, ducking her head and slipping quickly into the ladies' room. Blessed reprieve. This seduction business was hard work.

She splashed her heated face with cold water and told herself to calm down. She didn't have to do this if she didn't want to. It was just a game. A bit of fun. She'd always taken sex so seriously. It was time she learned to let down her hair a little and have a good time.

Especially when she'd be having that good time with

Quint. She thought about kissing him and her mouth went
dry. Oh, how she wanted to kiss him.

*Steady. Don't forget what you learned in class today.*
*Make him want you. Act like it's no big deal if you kiss*
*him or not.*

She looked at herself in the mirror, saw her pupils
dilated darkly with desire, felt the tremor of longing run
through her. Tonight couldn't come fast enough.

AFTER DINNER the members of the tour group met out in
front of the resort where, as promised, a flotilla of
gondolas awaited them. Music poured from the outdoor
speakers. "Bella Notte." People paired off two by two in
the gondolas and floated away down the canals.

Jorgie had spent an hour trying on one outfit after
another, struggling to find the right combination that
sent the message she wanted—easy come, easy go. She'd
finally settled on simple tailored black slacks that fit
snugly and a black-and-white vertically striped silk
V-neck blouse that showed just a whisper of cleavage
and black, strappy, two-inch sandals. Her jewelry was
muted. Gold stud earrings and a matching gold watch.
She'd bought a brighter color of lipstick than she
normally wore—Heartbreaker Red—at Maggie Cantrell's
suggestion.

She wore her hair down and ironed straight so it swung
past her shoulders. She could feel the heat of Quint's gaze
on her but she did not look over at him. The line dwindled.
More couples paired off. She waited a full five minutes
before lifting her head to meet his gaze.

The ardor in his eyes flattened her. This man wanted
*her.* The allure was compelling. She held his gaze but did
not smile when he smiled, but lifted her chin and canted

her head. She studied him with an indolent look, trying to convey that she was only mildly intrigued.

He bowed.

She nodded.

Whispered voices came from behind them, and that's when she realized his students were watching his every move. It unsettled her more than she expected. For one thing, Jorgie had completely forgotten she was supposed to be a plant. For another thing, she'd never been one to court the spotlight.

"May I have this ride?" he asked, and extended his hand as the next gondola in line bobbed up to the loading platform.

She panicked for a second, not knowing what to do. If she refused then she wouldn't get to ride with him. If she agreed it would look as if Casanova's seduction techniques were working.

Jorgie sniffed delicately. "I wouldn't mind," she said. "Until a better opportunity comes along."

Behind them, a guy guffawed.

Quint looked a bit befuddled by her reply, but he recovered quickly. "Thank you for agreeing to accompany me."

She didn't answer, nor did she take his hand as she climbed into the boat. Instead, she held her palm out to the gondolier, who helped her inside.

Quint seated himself beside her. He smelled delicious. She darted her tongue out to lick her lips, but stopped herself.

The gondolier stuck his oar in the water and they were off, skimming gracefully across the water. The moon climbed the sky. The night breeze blew cool for midsummer. Quint's knee was so close to hers. Jorgie could hardly believe she was in Venice, living her dream of embarking on a wild sexual fling.

They glided underneath a bridge. People along the walkway overhead stared down at them. "Yo, Casanova," someone called down. "You gonna kiss her or what?"

"One of your students?" Jorgie asked drily.

He gave her a lopsided smile. "Sorry about that."

"You may kiss me if you wish," she said, making sure she kept control of the situation. She leaned in close, and then paused for a moment. "For the sake of your reputation."

He lowered his eyelids. "Nah, I think I'll wait."

That flummoxed her a bit. He'd looked so eager, she'd thought...

*Cool it. He's not Casanova. He's just putting on a show for his students. Remember he asked you to be the plant because you were someone he could never fall in love with.*

That thought took all the wind from her sails. She turned her head and was alarmed to find a salty lump in her throat.

The gondolier picked up singing "Bella Notte" in a deep-throated Italian voice. In spite of her best intentions to keep tight control on her emotions, Jorgie felt herself swept away by the romance of Venice.

Quint slipped an arm around her. Jorgie shot him a quelling glare even as her breathing sped up. "What?" he asked. "Too soon?"

The line she toed was a fine one. She wanted to encourage him, but only slightly. Give him hope, but not much promise. She gave a bored sigh and looked away, much like Lady Evangeline must have done with the real Casanova, but inside Jorgie's heart pounded a twitchy tempo.

The gondolier switched to "Clair de Lune" as they

entered the Grand Canal thronged with gondolas. The air tasted of enchantment, impossibly sweet, and Quint's masculine scent dizzied her senses.

"This feels so magical," she whispered, forgetting to be Lady Evangeline for a second. She was all Jorgie, the girl next door who'd spent a chunk of her girlhood fantasizing about the alluring devil-may-care man beside her. She'd imagined scenarios just like this one many times. To have him here seemed so surreal, as if she'd somehow managed to step into her own daydream.

But she wasn't really "here with him" here with him. She was playing a part, helping him with his class. This wasn't about a romantic evening with a man she was quickly discovering she still had a crush on.

*All the more reason to act like Lady Evangeline and keep him on his toes.*

"Live the magic," Quint murmured.

She hadn't noticed he'd been inching his body closer, but now she saw his thigh pressed against hers and his hand had slipped from her shoulders to her waist, and that he was reaching up with his other hand to gently stroke her cheek before sliding it down to tilt her chin upward.

He gazed into her eyes. He was going to kiss her. She should move. Lady Evangeline would have moved. But Jorgie was gobsmacked. By the singing gondolier, by the Grand Canal, by the full moon rising into the sky, by the dark water and the summer breeze and Quint, Quint, Quint.

Slowly, she closed her eyes, puckered her lips and waited. And when his mouth touched hers, she understood the true appeal of Casanova.

He made a woman feel cherished and adored.

# 7

_Prime a woman right and she'll gush for you_
_—Make Love Like Casanova_

QUINT'S KISS wove a spell over her as magical as the Venetian night—intoxicating, potent, mind-bending.

He tugged her tightly against his chest and she did not resist. Oh, who was she kidding? She wrapped her arms around his neck and kissed him right back. Their mouths locked, oblivious to the gondolier chuckling above them.

Jorgie parted her teeth, letting him slide his tongue inside. The flavor of him, all tingling and pepperminty, filled her mouth and made her long to throw decorum to the wind and pull him down on top of her in the bottom of the boat. She'd never had such wild impulses before. What was it about him that sparked her biological bacchanal that no other man had ever sparked? Quint embodied the sweetest of fantasies, and she luxuriated in it, tasting it juicy as a ripe peach.

The water lapped softly against the side of the gondola like the swift swoosh of a fevered heartbeat. The ruffling breeze rippled over her bare skin and she felt the hush of twilight settle into her soul.

She took a deep breath, smelled the Grand Canal and

Quint—all fresh air and clean skin and the mossy trace of dark water.

He kissed as the most accomplished of lovers, filled with passion and audacity and excitement. His kiss transfused those qualities into her.

What was this magic he had about him? It wasn't that he used his tongue in any special way, although the tickle of it against the roof of her mouth set her toes to tingling. The pressure of his lips was firm, but not too hard, nothing earth-shattering, when you got down to it. How come it felt so exceptional?

The strum of his tongue was gentle and unhurried. Exploring, but not exceeding boundaries the way some men did. He wasn't intent on doing a tonsillectomy. He just teased and cajoled, tempting with a featherlight touch that intrigued. And he seemed to be truly enjoying the way she melted into him, her responsiveness fueling his own. He acted as if he could kiss her all day and never come up for air.

His arms tightened around her, his chest felt hard against her soft breasts. Blood surged through her veins, pounded against her eardrums in the rhythm of a timeless mating ritual. Arousal was a speeding bullet shooting through her faster than anything she'd ever experienced. Instantly, she was hot and horny and hungering for him in a way she'd never hungered for another. For sure she'd never felt this sharp, physical urgency with Brian.

Or anyone else, for that matter.

She'd had no idea she could feel like this. So wild and wanton and out of control. Where had it come from, this stark, primal need?

Full-throttle lust caused her to throb and ache in every molecule of her body until she was pulsing with it—her collarbone, her throat, her shins. Her skin burned, hot and jittery. Her breasts swelled heavy and sensitive against the scratchy lace of her bra and she flushed hot all over. Not just her skin now, but she was sizzling on a cellular level—fevered, delirious, burning up with need.

He slipped a warm hand up underneath her shirt, splayed it over her belly, all the while still kissing her. Jorgie swallowed back a moan of pleasure.

*You can't give in this easily. If you want to win him, then you have to make him work for it.* The voice in her head dished out advice à la Lady Evangeline.

She leaned back, broke the kiss, and encircled his wrist with her fingers, stopping his hand from edging higher. Her mouth, wet from his kiss, cooled in the night breeze, breaking her out of the magical spell, snapping her back to reality.

"Wait," she said, shocked that her voice sounded so pleading, as if she were actually begging him to continue.

His fingers drummed lightly against her stomach, playing her like a keyboard, distracting her.

She shook her head. "Stop."

His hand stilled but he did not remove it from underneath her shirt. "Is that really what you want?" he asked in a dozy, dreamy voice as if he'd been just as caught up in the fantasy as she had.

"Please," she whimpered, and hated herself for begging, "move your hand."

Slowly, he extracted his hand, drawing up his fingers, gliding away from her skin. Part of her ached to just say "what the hell" and invite him up to her room when they got back to the villa, but part of her knew if she gave in to him now she wouldn't be any different from all the other women he'd known, eager and ready to be bedded.

The gondolier had stopped singing and she noticed for

the first time they'd left the Grand Canal and were headed back to the villa. She heard water lapping against the boat with each stroke of the oar.

"What's going on here, Quint?"

The moonlight bathed his face in a blue-white glow. Amusement flashed in his eyes. "We're enjoying a magical evening."

"There's only one thing wrong with magic," she said.

He narrowed his gaze. "What's that?"

"It's not real."

"It's real for now."

She let out her breath and it was only then she realized she'd been holding it. "Is this about your class? About your Casanova techniques, or is this about Quint and Jorgie?"

He looked her in the eye. "It's about both, I guess."

"I'm confused."

"Casanova is part of the fantasy. So is Venice."

"That's the part that scares me," she said. "I'm a realist at heart. I don't know if I can ride on the coattails of whim and let the winds take me where they may. I don't know if I can be your plant without my emotions getting involved."

He shrugged and she felt it inside of her, as if she were shrugging, too. How was that possible? "You have your whole life to be steeped in reality, Jorgie. Can't you just take this vacation as it comes? That's what Eros is all about, you know. I thought that was why you came here."

In all honesty, she didn't really know why she was here. Mostly, it was because Avery had bought her a ticket and put her on the plane.

"I guess I'm wondering what happens when I get home."

"You look back on this trip with fond memories."

"That's it?"

"Why does it need to be more?" He leaned away from her, the skittish movement of a carefree man who was being asked to examine his values. "Are you looking for commitment? I thought you recently got out of a relationship."

Jorgie sighed. "I'm not looking for happily ever after. I'm not even sure if I'm looking for anything at all. Still, I don't take romantic liaisons lightly."

He laughed then, cocked an eyebrow. "'Romantic liaisons?'"

"Okay, so I spent too much time in the eighteenth century this morning." She smiled.

He leaned in again, closing the gap he'd created, and grinned at her, his white teeth gleaming in the darkness. "It's okay, Jorgie. You don't have to do anything you don't want to do. If the fantasy isn't fun, then don't go there."

But it was fun. That was the problem. She didn't know how to have fun. She didn't know how to relax and let go. She didn't know how to be casual when it came to sex. "Do you still want me to be your plant?"

"Not if it makes you uncomfortable."

She bit her bottom lip. "I do want to help you."

"I'd appreciate it, but again, I don't want you to do something you're not excited about."

"I'm excited. Though it's all getting confused in my head. What's real? What's fantasy? What's a game? What's the truth?"

In all honesty, she wanted this. Wanted him. But she feared a broken heart. She was still ragged after Brian's betrayal, even though she was quickly figuring out she hadn't truly been in love with him. How did you know what love really was? And was it anything more than just a chemical reaction? Was romantic love itself the fantasy? One that Casanova had spent his life chasing? And how closely related was Quint to that famous lover on an emotional level?

She considered telling him she'd changed her mind, that she would love to come up to his room and spend the night having hot, sweaty sex with no consequences or repercussions or expectations. But she thought of Lady Evangeline and how she'd kept Casanova on a string by never fully giving in to him. The thought made her smile. How wicked it was to tease.

The gondola gave a bump against the landing, signaling that they'd arrived at the Eros villa. Quint got out first, and then reached down a hand to help her disembark. She took his hand because she needed his guidance, but steeled herself against the onslaught of desire his touch created.

"Well," she said, once she was on the cobblestone pathway beside him.

"Well," he echoed.

The moment was awkward. She couldn't think of anything to say that would smooth it over. The evening was finished. This was good-night.

And yet, she longed to linger.

In fact, she was hoping for another kiss.

"Would you care for a nightcap in the resort's bar?" he asked hopefully.

"I don't think that would be such a—"

"Please, say yes," he interrupted. "My students are watching and they're expecting some serious Casanova moves."

Jorgie glanced over to see a flock of young men gathered on the bridge near the entrance to the resort. They were watching Quint with knowing grins. She rolled her eyes.

"I'll owe you big time," he said.

"All right," she conceded. "But only one drink and then I'm going to bed."

He grinned.

"Alone," she added with emphasis.

AFTER HER NIGHTCAP with Quint, where she flirted and batted her eyes for the benefit of his students who'd followed them into the bar, she allowed him to walk her to her room.

They stood in the hallway gazing into each other's eyes. She wanted to say "ah, the heck with it" and invite him inside, but she knew she couldn't. Not if she didn't want to be just another one of Quint Mason's conquests.

She said good-night, and when he leaned in for a kiss, she gathered up all the control she had in her, turned her back on him and slid her key card through the contraption on the door. It flashed green. She opened the door and turned back to him, blocking the entrance with her body, and held out her hand. "Well, good night."

"A handshake?" Quint chuckled.

"A handshake," she confirmed.

"You're killing me here, Jorgie."

"We had an agreement. One nightcap and I was going to bed alone." Then she gave him a sly smile and backed inside. Just as she shut the door, she heard a ding in the hallway as the elevator settled onto her floor.

"Hey, Casanova," she heard a young man call out. "Looks like you struck out."

She stopped the door before it closed completely, and cocked her head, listening to the exchange.

"I didn't strike out, lads," Quint said as he headed down the corridor in their direction. "This is merely stage one in a grand seduction. It's called priming the pump. Move too fast and you'll come up dry. But prime a woman right and she'll gush for you."

A snap of anger crackled through her and she slammed the door. Loudly. Of all the arrogant, chauvinistic things to say…

*Calm down, he was only saying it for his students.*

This whole role-playing thing was making her feel jerked around by her emotions. Did she want to go to bed with him or not? Did she want to learn how to have great sex?

She plunked down on the bed and kicked off her shoes. She couldn't sort this out by herself. She needed someone to talk to. Mind swirling, she dug her cell phone from her purse and called Avery.

"Yo." Avery answered on the second ring. "S'up?"

"Is this a good time?"

"You mean am I having wild monkey sex with a hunky guy, then no. I can talk."

"But you said one guy had caught your eye?"

"Oh, one caught it, all right," Avery said. "But he seems immune. I'm in the bungalow next to his, so I did a little striptease with the blinds open and—"

"Avery! You did not."

"I did, but don't worry, dear Prudence, it didn't work. He saw me, I know he did, but the next day he acted like nothing had happened. He must be gay," she mused.

"Or he's not the type of guy who takes advantage of horny women on vacation."

"Excuse me, but all guys are that type of guy."

"You can't paint everyone with the same brush. Some people just don't possess the same sexual drive you do."

"Poor them," Avery said. "So what's going on with you? Did you get a chance to talk to Quint?"

"Honestly, I wish you were here. I'm feeling a bit over-whelmed." Jorgie paced the floor and unbuttoned her blouse, the cell phone cradled between her chin and her shoulder.

"Hmm, I'm sensing you had the opportunity to take him to bed and you turned him down."

"I had to."

"How come?"

Jorgie told her the story of Lady Evangeline and Casanova and how she was playing the part of his love interest.

"Woman, that's just wacked. You realize if you keep playing the part of this Lady Evangeline you're not going to get any."

"I know, but I'm not sure I want to get any if it means I'll just be another notch on Quint's bedpost."

"Are you saying you want something more from him than sex?"

"No. Yes. I don't know."

"Which is it really?"

"Okay, I want sex with him but I'm afraid that if I go to bed with Quint then I will want more and I don't know how to stop myself from wanting more." She hung her blouse in the closet.

"So tell me exactly what happened."

"We went on a gondola ride."

"How was that?"

"The most romantic thing I've ever done."

"Uh-oh. That's a problem right there. Stop thinking in terms of romance. Say it was the hottest thing you ever did."

"But it wasn't. It was romantic."

"Then stop doing romantic things."

Jorgie stepped out of her pants and hung them beside her blouse. "I'm in Venice, the most romantic city on the face of the earth. How am I supposed to do that?"

"You're working yourself up into a fuss the way you always do," Avery said.

"I don't." Jorgie unhooked her bra.

"You do, and here's the reason why. You find it impossible to live in the moment. You're always thinking about the future, borrowing trouble for some time that's not even here yet. Well, what if you just found out you were going to die tomorrow? Would you sleep with Quint then?"

She didn't even have to think about it. "Absolutely."

"So there's your answer. Shag the guy until you're blue in the face."

Jorgie paused to pull the phone from her ear long enough to slide the bra off her shoulders and slip into her sleep shirt. "You make it sound so easy."

"That's because it is. Follow your instincts, not your brain. Your brain will trip you up every time."

"You think I should do it?"

"Do you feel safe with him?"

"No question."

"Then just go for it. Forget this Lady Evangeline crap. It's ancient history and it might not even be true. Besides, right now is all that any of us really have. And even if it wasn't, even if you had sex with Quint and in spite of all your best intentions you fell in love with him and then he broke your heart, isn't it better to have loved and lost than never to have loved at all?"

QUINT COULDN'T SLEEP. He could still taste Jorgie on his tongue. Still smell her lovely scent in his nostrils, could still feel the effects of her in his body. The erection he'd gotten in the gondola hadn't fully abated.

He left the villa and walked the cobblestones of Venice at midnight. For once, the streets were mostly empty. There were a few couples strolling hand in hand or kissing in the moonlight. There were one or two drunks staggering out of bars, but for the most part, he was alone with his thoughts.

Quint didn't like being alone with his thoughts.

Water lapped against the rocks. Gondolas bobbed at their moorings. He jammed his hands into his pockets; his fingers brushed against his cell phone. Jake. He could call Jake and talk about the threats made against Taylor Milton and her resorts. That ought to keep his mind off Jorgie Gerard.

"Hey, man," he said when Jake picked up the phone.

"Mason," Jake said in his clipped, all-business tone. Anyone listening to him would never guess that he and Quint had been friends since college, had served in the air force together for four years. He was as reserved as Quint was open. Most people would assume they had nothing in common and on the surface, they did not. But their shared military experience had bound them in a way nothing else could have. Their styles complemented each other. Quint was the graceful charmer, Jake the street-savvy tough guy.

"How are things in La-la Land?"

"Too much damned sunshine." Jake grunted. He'd been raised in Seattle and rain was as much a part of him as his taciturn nature.

"Any action on your end?"

"You talking about business or women?"

"Whatever kind of action you're getting, let's hear it."

"Quiet on the sabotage front."

"Nothing at all?"

"A chair broken in the dining hall at lunch when a hefty guy sat in it, but I think it's safe to assume it wasn't sabotage."

They'd been on this case for months now, and after the bomb that had been found in the Japanese resort, nothing else had surfaced until Taylor had received the letter. "Did Dougal tell you about the letter Taylor Milton got?"

"He faxed me a copy."

"What do you think?"

"Calm before the storm."

"That's what I was afraid of." Quint splayed a hand to the back of his neck. "Who do you think could be doing this?"

"My money's on a disgruntled employee, but I've been through the employee files with a fine-tooth comb, and nothing."

"Same here. Maybe it's the competition. Like that airline Dougal's fiancée worked for. What was it called?"

"Getaway Airlines, but Dougal's put the owner, Porter Langely, through the wringer and he came up empty-handed. I hope something happens soon because I'm bored out of my skull here."

"Really? I kind of like it."

"Well, sure, you get to play Casanova. Right up your alley."

"Hey, you get to film beautiful women all day."

"They're not all beautiful. This morning I filmed a seventy-two-year-old woman and her boyfriend. I mean, it's nice to see they still have the spark, but it's kind of tough to get a glimpse into your future, wrinkles, sags and all."

"So how are things on the romantic front?"

"Ah," Jake said. "Your favorite topic."

"Anything shaking for you?"

"I have two words for you, Mason. Morality clause. We signed one. Remember that?"

"Oh, yeah, like Dougal himself didn't violate it when he fell for Roxie," he said, referring to Dougal's fiancée. Dougal had met her while undercover at the Eros resort in England.

"Well, he's the boss, you're not."

"We're not in the military anymore. You can let go of the rank thing."

"He writes our checks. That's good enough for me."

"How do you have so much control?"

"Pure thoughts," Jake said flippantly.

Quint laughed. "I don't believe that for a minute."

"So I take it you're having women troubles?"

"Not women, woman. But it's no big deal, really. One gondola ride, that's all."

Jake hooted. "She wouldn't put out for you."

He felt slightly embarrassed that he was that easy to predict, and the fact that a woman had not eagerly gone back to his room with him was so unusual.

"When was the last time that happened?" Jake asked.

"I can't remember," he mumbled.

"I can. It was sophomore year of college. Jenny Gray. She was saving herself for marriage and she drove you crazy. You were consumed with her for months."

"Was not."

"Dude, I was there."

"'Dude'?"

"Oh, shit, I've been in California too long, they've got me saying it now. Wish this saboteur would strike so we could catch the guy and I could get the hell out of here."

"So anyway, what am I supposed to do about this woman?"

"Stop obsessing about her because she didn't give it up for you."

"But how?"

"Find someone else to distract you. Preferably a woman who isn't an Eros guest."

"Yeah, yeah, you're right," Quint said, but he didn't

want to be distracted. All he wanted to do was be with Jorgie, whether she had sex with him or not.

And that realization scared the living hell out of him.

# 8

_____

*It's all about the look*
*—Make Love Like a Movie Star*

FOR SEVEN EVENINGS RUNNING, Jake Stewart had been treated to his own private striptease. Night after night, Avery peeled off her clothes in the bedroom of the bungalow across the way. She never closed the blinds and she always took her time. He had to assume she knew he was watching.

But during the day, when he saw her around the resort, she acted as if nothing had happened, and her mysterious little game was driving him right over the edge of reason. Like now. He was in the elegant dining room having breakfast with a group of cameramen and Avery sauntered toward their table. She looked straight ahead, tray in her arms, and never turned her head in his direction, but as she passed the narrow aisle between the tables her hip brushed lightly against his back.

Had it been accidental? Or calculated?

Instantly, the moisture in his mouth evaporated and his cock hardened. Someone at the table must have said something funny because everyone was laughing, but Jake hadn't heard a word. He faked a chuckle and tried to concentrate on what his colleagues were laughing about, but the only thing he was aware of was the spot on his back where her body had grazed his.

After being exposed—quite literally—to Avery Bodel and having the sight of her naked body burned into his retinas, he feared there was only one way to ease his burgeoning appetite and get his mind back on work.

Damn his code of ethics—and that morals clause he'd signed—that prevented him from mixing business and pleasure. Besides, he and Avery? Oil versus water.

He blew out his breath and chanced a look over his shoulder to see if he could find where she'd gone. Two attractive young blondes barely over eighteen wriggled their fingers at him, then put their heads together, lowered their lashes coyly and giggled.

What the hell was going on around here? Had someone put a Seduce Me sign on his back? Even though he didn't consider himself particularly good-looking, certainly not like his buddy, Quint, he'd had his share of women. But he'd never received this many flirtatious overtures in such a short period of time. It had to be the Make Love Like A Movie Star venue. They must all be trying out the new techniques they'd learned.

Each tour started with the guests spending the first several days attending acting classes, touring the studios and being fitted for wardrobes. The last half of their vacations consisted of starring in their own romantic movie, scripted especially for them (or they could chose to reenact scenes from their favorite romantic movie) to indulge their secret fantasies, but only up to a point. The movies had to stay R-rated, no crossing the lines into X-rated territory. However, the guests were allowed to rent cameras from the resort for their own bedroom play and in those instances, what they did behind closed doors was their business.

Most people who came on this tour were with spouses or significant others. But a few came alone. For those guests, actors were hired to play the love interest. The last tour had finished up their movies yesterday and today this current group started filming. He wondered if he would be on the crew of Avery's movie or if he'd luck out and get some happily married, middle-aged couple to shoot.

Jake shook his head and got up. Filming started at eight and he needed thirty minutes' prep time.

He arrived on the set along with the rest of the crew and went straight to the camera to set up the opening shot. The stagehands were already at work. Usually, the stage held a bed, but this morning, the bed had been replaced with a bathtub.

The director came onto the set, followed by his assistants, all flitting about, creating a pretty fantasy for rich people who thought nothing of plunking down cash to indulge their sexual fantasies. This glossy, insular world was a long way from the things he'd seen and done in Afghanistan. Things he'd never fully overcome.

He made adjustments to the camera, mentally shutting out the bustle around him, and wondered what it would be like to see the world as one big playground, nothing but fun and games and good times. No starving mothers. No children maimed by land mines. No men so consumed by misguided fervor they didn't care who they killed in the process.

Satisfied that he had all the settings in order, he went through the script, checking out the shots he'd need for the scene. It was pretty straightforward. They were filming the bathtub scene from *Pretty Woman* with some variations to the script that the guest had requested, including a seductive, partial striptease. Immediately, Jake thought of the private stripteases Avery had been doing for him. He had to put her out of his mind. He had work to do. Both as a cameraman and as an undercover air marshal turned body-guard for Taylor Milton's resort. From now on, he was keeping his blinds tightly closed. If Avery wanted to continue her nightly stripteases, she'd have to do it without his participation.

Then the side door opened and Avery walked out onto the stage dressed in a bathrobe, fishnet stockings and four-inch black stilettos.

AVERY HAD REQUESTED Jake as her cameraman. She was normally quite bold and had no trouble letting her needs be known. She was not shy or retiring, but suddenly, once she was on the stage and met Jake's eyes, her bravado evaporated.

What had she been thinking asking for him to be the cameraman on her movie? She'd been trying for the last seven nights to drive the man crazy with sexual desire and either she wasn't doing something right or he simply was not interested in her.

He wasn't involved with someone else. She'd already asked around. Maybe he was pining for an old love?

*Or maybe he's just not that into you.*

When she'd brushed against him in the dining room, he hadn't made a single twitch. The man had amazing self-control. She bit down on her bottom lip just thinking about it.

"Lights! Camera! Action!"

The minute the director said those words everyone on the sound stage sprang into motion, leaving Avery blinking into Jake's camera. She couldn't get past the fact he was there watching her, filming her. The lighting crew turned the lights on soft focus. The guy holding the boom mike positioned it over the bathtub where she would soon slide in and assume her role of Vivian, the sweet-natured hooker from *Pretty Woman*.

The tip of her nose itched, but she didn't dare scratch it. *Don't think about your nose, don't think about Jake, just enjoy this once-in-a-lifetime opportunity to be the star of your own version of the famous Cinderella story.*

"Wait a minute," someone called from off the set.

"Cut." The director sighed and looked irritated. "What is it?"

The crew member went over to whisper something into the director's ear.

"Seriously?" The director shook his head.

Avery shaded her eyes against the glare of the spotlights. "Is something wrong?"

The director smiled brightly at her. "We're taking a short break."

"Is there a problem I should know about?" she asked, a knot of anxiety rising in her throat.

"Just some production difficulties. We'll be back in a minute. Tia, could you get Avery something to drink while she's waiting?"

The assistant hustled to do his bidding, while the director turned to Jake. "Stewart," he said, "I need to see you outside."

"The actor we hired for this script got a bad burrito in the cantina," the director, Tim Granger, said. "We need someone to fill in for him."

Jake stared at the man who kept raking his fingers through his graying goatee. "What?"

"All our actors are currently booked. We don't have

time to get a temp in here. You know the script. You're good-looking enough to play her leading man, and I can get Felicity to fill in for you behind the camera."

Jake shook his head. His place was behind the camera, watching. He was undercover. Being in the limelight was a stupid idea. Never mind that being that close to Avery would test every ounce of self-control he possessed. Jake shook his head. "Not a good idea."

"Come on, dude," Tim said. "Take one for the team. You're not married, right?"

"I'm not."

"And purple hair aside, she *is* gorgeous."

"Her looks aren't the issue."

"What is the issue?"

"I don't like being in front of the camera."

"Get over it." Tim growled. "This woman has paid a lot of money to have her every fantasy fulfilled and you're going to fulfill it. Get to wardrobe and makeup, now."

"But…"

"Just do it."

Realizing he had little choice in the matter, Jake stormed into wardrobe. He couldn't decide what he was angry about, but he was mad. And then as he sat in the makeup chair getting his face dusted with powder to make it less shiny under the lights, something unexpected occurred to him.

He wasn't angry. He was scared.

Damn! What was he so scared of?

It was a rhetorical question because he knew the answer. He was scared of the uncontrollable urges that struck him every time he was around Avery. He didn't like this. Not at all.

Thirty minutes later, he was backstage while the director told Avery to begin her striptease.

He could see her in profile slowly ease the bathrobe off her shoulders. A wave of sensual heat shot through him, clean and deadly as a bullet. Jake sucked in a breath as his cock stiffened against his zipper.

*Get a grip. You can't go out there with a boner.*

He tried thinking unsexy thoughts, but there was no way he could think of anything but sliding his big hands down Avery's slender body. Not when the lowering of her bathrobe kept exposing more and more skin.

"Keep it R-rated," Tim Granger called out and gave instructions to Felicity, who was manning Jake's camera to hone in on Avery's legs while she completely dropped the towel and stepped into the warm bubble bath.

Every muscle in his body tensed as he watched her lower herself into the steamy water. She wore a tiger-print thong bikini, but still, it was itty bitty and showed off the glorious body nature had given her.

All the air leaked from his lungs and he pulled his palm down his face, searching for some semblance of control. But his self-restraint had gone AWOL, leaving him aching and hungry for this woman he barely knew.

"Go." One of the stage hands gave him a push. "You're on."

THE IMPACT of Jake's presence on the stage sent Avery's normally daring spirit packing. She felt tongue-tied and owl-eyed. If Jorgie were here, she'd have a good laugh.

Jake sent her a look that dizzied her head. He stared at her as if she was the only woman on earth and he was the only man and the survival of the species depended on them having sex *now*.

Avery gulped.

He came toward her, holding up the towel as she slipped

out of the bathtub. She could feel the heat of his gaze burning up her skin. He wrapped the towel around her and then his arms were around her, as well, the rolled-up sleeves of his white button-down shirt soaking up the water dripping from the ends of her hair.

His mouth closed over hers as he pulled her damp body flush against his chest. The kiss was in the script, but it felt completely unscripted and frankly, he knocked the pins out from under her. He tilted her chin with the hand that wasn't wrapped tightly around her waist and kissed her with an open, greedy kiss so hungry it sucked all the breath from her lungs.

Avery parted her lips and his tongue slipped deeper into her mouth, running over her tongue in unabashed command. She'd thought because he liked to watch, because he hid behind a camera, that he was not a dominant, demanding guy. How wrong she'd been.

She sank against his hard body, both startled and pleased by this new revelation. His erection pushed against her belly, leaving no doubt about his interest. Luckily, his back was to the camera, so the glaring evidence of his arousal wasn't being filmed. He made her feel desired and wanted. It was a heady sensation.

With a soft moan, she wrapped her arms around his neck, forgetting all about the camera, the crew, the movie. Only one thing dominated her mind—*Jake, Jake, Jake.*

She pressed herself against him, trying desperately to get closer. His mouth was still on hers, firm and inquisitive. Her sex tightened, moistening, readying for his invasion.

He splayed a palm over her rump, only the terry cloth material coming between skin-to-skin contact. Her nipples hardened in response, beading up tight, and her breath slipped from her lungs in short, escalating gasps.

Gently, he grazed her nipple, knotted stiff beneath the oversize bath towel, with the back of his hand. A sweet stinging sensation shot like a lightning bolt from her nipple to her groin, bathing her in physical awareness.

He pulled back, breaking the kiss, and looked deeply into her eyes. An odd expression lurked in his hooded gaze—a combination of bafflement, lust, cynicism and irritation. His breathing was as hot and fast as hers.

If the director hadn't yelled "Cut!" Avery was certain he would have kissed her again and if he hadn't, she would have kissed him.

# 9

*Uncertainty is the key to keeping his interest*
*—Make Love Like a Courtesan*

FOR SEVEN DAYS, Jorgie did her best to keep Quint at arm's length while at the same time flirting madly with him as she was supposed to do. She made sure never to find herself alone with him, although it wasn't easy because he seemed hell-bent on courting her.

On the day after their gondola ride, he sent her a dozen purple orchids. She had no idea how he knew her favorite color was purple or that orchids were her favorite flowers. She wanted desperately to keep them, but knew that in her place Lady Evangeline would have sent them back to Casanova with a kind note telling him she could not accept his gift because it was too romantic.

The next day, he sent her a book of erotic love poems. She sent it back, as well.

The third day, he sent her a box of chocolates. This she accepted, one because she was in truth a chocaholic and two because it's how Lady Evangeline operated. She gave in just enough to keep Casanova hooked on her string. She heard through the grapevine that Quint crowed victoriously to his class that his techniques had battered down her defenses. But that night, at the Venetian ball, she refused to dance with him, leaving Quint looking totally befuddled.

At eight a.m. on the seventh day, both the Make Love Like Casanova and the Make Love Like A Courtesan students were scheduled to visit the island of Murano and take a private tour of a glassblowing factory. As they entered the water taxi, Jorgie held back, letting the rest of the group surge ahead of her and provide a protective shield between her and Quint.

She'd just sat down and was looking out across the lagoon, enjoying the cool morning breeze ruffling her hair, when she felt someone sit beside her. She didn't have to look up to know it was Quint. His unique scent teased her nose.

"Hey," he said.

She glanced over at him but didn't say a word, just ducked her head, studied him through lowered lashes and tried to ignore the erratic pounding of her heart.

"You've been avoiding me." His deep voice rumbled near her ear.

"You flatter yourself if you believe that I give you that much thought," Jorgie said, trying to sound glib and carefree. Actually, she was trying to imitate Avery. Glib and carefree did not come naturally to Jorgie.

He gave her a wry, crooked smile that lit up his handsome features and splayed both palms—one on top of the other—over his heart. "You wound me."

"I seriously doubt that."

"You treat my heart so cavalierly. I do have feelings, you know, and when it comes to you, I have trouble controlling myself."

Strange emotions lumped up in her throat, knotted her

chest. She stared at him, taken off guard. He sounded so sincere. She'd been attracted to him at thirteen; she was even more attracted to him now. She'd been fighting the decade-old attraction for the last seven days, but with that admission and his devastatingly adorable grin, her resolve shattered. The power of his smile set her head spinning.

Or maybe it was just the speed of the water taxi. That was it. Motion-induced dizziness. He wasn't responsible at all for this blurry, breathless sensation taking hold of her.

She leaned forward and rested her forearms on the side of the boat in an attempt to steady herself. But he followed suit, mimicking her movements, and his elbow bumped against her, firm and fundamental and so hot she felt herself melting like ice cream in the sun.

"This is fun, huh?" He grinned at her. "Being here with an old friend. The romance of Venice."

"Fun," she echoed, but the feelings churning inside her were far from fun. They were scary and exciting and nerve-racking and about as much fun as dangling from tenterhooks.

"Venice is one of my most favorite places on earth," he said, his voice a low rumble in his throat.

It made her think of motorcycles and how afraid of them she was. Jorgie shifted away from his distracting elbow, sliding her arms down the smooth fiberglass of the vaporetto. She couldn't form a coherent thought when he was touching her. Oh, this was bad.

"You've been here often?" she asked.

"I was stationed at Aviano air base. It's only an hour away."

"Really? I never knew you were stationed in Italy."

"For a year."

"Do you speak Italian?"

*"Sì, parlo un piccolo italiano."*

"What was her name?"

*"Che cosa?"* he asked.

"Huh?"

"What?"

"What, what?"

"Okay, have we got a Who's On First thing going on here."

"The name of the woman," Jorgie said. "That you used to come see in Venice. What was her name?"

He grinned. "How do you know there was a woman?"

"With you, there's always a woman."

"It's the Italian way."

"And yet, you're not the least bit Italian."

"I take the slogan 'when in Rome do as the Romans do' quite literally."

"We're not in Rome."

"No," he said as the vaporetto bumped gently against the dock. "We're in Murano."

"So we are." She stood.

"Gia."

"What?"

"Now you're doing it." He looked at her with sultry eyes and got to his feet along with the rest of the passengers. "The girl I used to visit, her name was Gia."

"Do you still keep in touch?"

"No." His look was pure Casanova. "Her husband is the jealous type."

Jealousy brushed against her, as well. This was stupid, being jealous over his ex-girlfriend, and yet she couldn't help how she felt. "Was she married when you used to see her?"

He made a disgruntled noise. "What do you take me for?"

"A rogue."

"I like to have a good time, but I'm not in the habit of busting up marriages."

"It's good to know you have some standards," she said.

"You're jealous," he teased.

"I am not."

"Then why are your cheeks turning pink?"

She raised her hands to her cheeks. "They're not."

"Gotcha." He laughed.

"Ass."

"Princess."

"Jerk."

"Sweetheart."

"You're infuriating."

"And you're fun to rile."

"Seriously, these moves work on other women?"

"Nope, these are the moves I've come up with just for you." He winked.

Oh, it was stupid, but that made her feel special. *He's lying. Don't buy in to it. He wants you to feel special.*

During their exchange, everyone else had filed off the boat, leaving them the last ones to exit. Quint got out ahead of her and then reached down to help her out of the boat. She didn't want to take his hand, but the dock looked slippery and she'd already seen one woman stumble. She didn't know which was the lesser of two evils—taking the risk of a fall, or touching him.

Warily, she extended her palm.

His hand enveloped hers.

Their gazes met, wedded.

She shivered in response and almost yanked her hand

back, but he was already pulling her up on the dock beside him. What was going on here? Why was she letting this physical chemistry between them get the better of her?

"Here we are," he murmured.

The attraction was burning too hotly, moving too fast, zooming beyond anything she could control. He was a one-man wrecking ball, crashing through all her defenses with his wickedly sexy grin.

"We're getting left behind," he warned, still holding on to her hand.

She wanted to pull away, but it felt so darn good. Just a minute longer, she told herself, and allowed him to lead her over the cement walkway toward a cluster of buildings lining the main thoroughfare. The tour guide walked ahead of the group, detailing the history of Murano. She tilted her head, trying to get her focus on what he was saying and off the feel of Quint's calloused palm against her smooth one.

"Murano," said the guide, "is a glassmaker's paradise. The glassmaking industry was moved from Venice in 1291 because most of the structures were made of wood and glassmaking is a heat-intensive endeavor. Fearing fires that could destroy the city, the town elders decided Murano was the perfect place to relocate."

They crested a small hill that descended down into the middle of town. Seagulls winged overhead, calling to each other in their querulous voices. Vegetables, housed in wooden crates, were set up at vendors' stands overflowing with tomatoes, onions, artichokes, bell peppers and truffles. She could almost taste the tang of antipasto. Flowers of all colors and shapes bloomed gloriously in window boxes—jasmine, crocuses, bluebell, periwinkle and violets. The sweet, heady smell filled her nostrils as they strolled past.

But as the guide led the tour south, Quint, with his hand still wrapped around hers, steered Jorgie north.

"Where are you taking me?" she demanded, trying to pull her hand away, but he stubbornly held on.

"Do you want the tourist version of glassblowing?" he asked. "Or would you like to participate in the real thing?"

"What do you mean?"

"Stick with me, kid, and the world will be your oyster."

"I don't like oysters," she teased, merely to be petulant. Truthfully, she was a bit unnerved that he was cutting her off from the herd. Not that she was afraid of him. Rather, it was her own impulses that frightened her. Alone was not a good place to be with Quint. Not when he made her feel the way he made her feel.

"You'll like this," he reassured her. "Trust me."

She glanced back over her shoulder as the other group grew smaller in the distance. *Help.*

They approached a building made of red brick. The door stood open. The weathered sign over the door read Veneziani Glass Shop. A young man stood outside, sweeping off the front stoop.

"Uberto!" Quint called.

The dark-haired young man looked up, then his face broke into a welcoming smile. "Ciao, Quint."

They embraced, pounding each other heartily on the back. Then Uberto pulled back, peppering Quint with questions in Italian. Quint nodded and smiled.

Jorgie had no idea what they were talking about, but she heard the name Gia mentioned and saw the young man rake a speculative glance over her.

"*Sì.*" Quint nodded and then motioned Jorgie over.

*"Buongiorno, mancanza."*

She knew enough guidebook Italian to realize he'd wished her a good morning. Jorgie smiled. *"Buongiorno."*

Uberto motioned them into the little shop. Once inside, her eyes were treated to a beautiful array of Murano hand-blown glass. She wanted to linger and admire the pieces with steep price tags, but Uberto was leading them through a door at the back of the shop.

"What's going on?" She leaned over to whisper to Quint.

"I've arranged private glassblowing lessons for you."

Pleased and flattered, she murmured, "Thank you."

The small shop opened up into a cavernous back room where the glassware was fired and formed. Two older men wearing sunglasses labored in the big room, handling white-hot glass with long metal tongs. The air carried a crisp, singed flavor that reminded her of sesame seed oil.

"The skill of glassblowing," Quint explained, "is over two thousand years old. It basically involves taking molten glass and inflating it. I'm going to lead you through a demonstration and then you're going to do it."

Jorgie blinked in surprise. "You know how to blow glass?"

"I do. Side benefit of dating Gia. Uberto is her cousin."

"You're full of surprises."

"Comes from a life well lived."

The men were fully focused on their work and could spare Quint little more than a simple hello. Their level of concentration was a marvel in and of itself.

"Molten glass is viscous, allowing you to blow it, and it gradually hardens as it cools. It takes a furnace temperature of 2,400 degrees Fahrenheit to transform the raw materials into glass," Quint explained. "The glass appears white-hot at this heat. Then the glass is left to 'fine out,' a step which allows the bubbles to rise from the mass, and then the working temp is lowered in the furnace to around 2,000 degrees. At this stage, it will turn bright orange."

She nodded, absorbing the details. He led her around the room, pointing out the techniques the glass smiths were using.

"Glassblowing involves three furnaces. The first is the crucible of molten glass." He pointed it out. "It's simply referred to as the furnace and this is where it all starts."

The heat radiating from the furnace warmed her skin, even from a respectful distance.

He motioned her over to a second furnace. "This is called the glory hole, and they use it to reheat a piece while they're working on it."

"Seriously? It's called the glory hole?"

His lips twitched. "Seriously."

Jorgie rolled her eyes. "A man must have come up with that moniker."

He laughed. "I'm sure you're right. Now this—" he paused and pointed out the third furnace "—is the annealer, and it's used to cool the glass over a period of several hours or days, depending on the size of the piece."

"Wow."

"So as you may have noticed, glassblowing is a lot like making love."

"Oh, please."

"You don't believe me?"

"No."

"They say glassblowers make the best lovers."

"Sounds like glassblower propaganda if you ask me."

"Furnace number one is like good foreplay," he murmured. "Turn up the heat and melt."

Jorgie swallowed.

"Step two, it's into the glory hole."

She nudged him with her elbow. "Pervert."

"Hey, I'm just saying." His grin was impish. "And then there's the afterglow of the annealer as things slowly cool down."

The truth was, as he talked she found herself heating up. He made an excellent point, but she wasn't about to tell him that. The man had enough of an ego as it was.

"So where does the blowing come in?" she asked.

"Let me demonstrate."

Her curiosity piqued, she watched him go through all the steps. His fingers were nimble on the blowpipe, and it was exciting to watch the glass inflate as he blew on the end. His calm patience amazed her. When the glass was too hot, he'd roll it against a metal table called a marver. When it cooled too quickly, he'd put it back in the glory hole for reheating. In the end he made a little cat of red glass.

Jorgie applauded his finished effort.

"For you," he said with a courtly bow. "I remember you like cats. Mr. Buttons was the name of your Siamese you had when you were a kid, right?"

She tilted her head. "You remember that?"

"I have a good memory for names." He picked the cat up with the tongs that he'd told her were called jacks. "And he goes into the annealer. It's a small piece so it should be ready for us to take back with us."

Uberto sauntered over. "You still have the touch," he said in heavily accented English.

"You taught me well."

"Is your lady ready for her lesson?" Uberto asked.

"Oh, I'm not his lady." Jorgie shook her head.

Uberto laughed and said something to Quint in Italian. Jorgie frowned. "What did he say?"

"He says you can't fool him. He sees the way your eyes light up when you look at me."

Jorgie punched him lightly on the forearm. "He did not."

"Can't pull one over on you, Ms. Gerard. Come on. You're going to make a vase."

"Um…" She cleared her throat. She wasn't sure about this.

"You can't chicken out now," Quint said.

She took a deep breath. She didn't know what unnerved her more—glassblowing or Quint.

"I'll help you."

That's exactly what she was afraid of.

"First, let's get you a Kevlar glove."

"You didn't use a glove."

"You're a beginner. Trust me, you'll want one."

Uberto appeared with the fire retardant glove and Jorgie slipped it onto her right hand.

"Pick a cold blowpipe," Quint instructed.

Jorgie did as he suggested, picking up a long narrow iron tube about an inch and a half in diameter.

"Now," he said, stepping across the room, "we go to the gathering tank."

She circled the tank, feeling radiating waves of intense heat wash over her.

"Here." He came up behind her. "Let me show you how to hold it."

His breath was warm against the nape of her neck as he repositioned her fingers on the cool metal rod. He wrapped his hands around hers and directed her forward with his leg. "Step up to the tank and set the pipe on the edge. Roll it against the side until you can see the reflection of the pipe on the surface of the molten glass. Be sure not to dip the blowpipe into the liquid glass. Just roll it over the surface."

Nervously, she inched forward with a death grip on the blowpipe. Sweat popped out on her forehead and she nibbled her bottom lip, paying close attention to everything he said, but acutely aware of the feel of his chest pressing against her back.

Inside the tank, the liquid glass glowed yellow; the heat fell over her face like a blanket. She saw the pipe's reflection in the glass as he'd said she would. His hand, still on hers, helped her slowly rotate the rod.

"Two complete revolutions," he said huskily.

She did as he asked. It was like turning apples in caramel.

"Now, carefully withdraw it."

She removed the blowpipe from the gathering tank. The viscous glass glowed bright amber as if she'd just gathered fiery honey. "I did it," she murmured joyfully. "Molten glass."

"Good job," he said. "But we're only getting started. Now over to the marver."

She carried the blowpipe to the marver. When she reached it, Quint's arms went around Jorgie's again as he helped her roll the glass into an even, on-center cylinder.

"Okay." His voice was low, steady. "Blow into the end of the pipe and cover the hole with your thumb to trap the air inside."

She put her lips to the now warm metal and blew softly, then obstructed the end with her thumb. Slowly, a bubble of glass began to inflate on the other end of the rod.

"Back to the gathering tank for more glass."

She collected more glass to the bubble and repeated the steps until Quint told her she had enough glass for the vase.

"Time for the optic mold." He picked up a heavy, vase-shaped cylinder and set it on the ground. Uberto brought over a step stool and placed it next to the cylinder. "You're going to be using the mold because it's most forgiving for beginners," Quint said. "Otherwise you'd use wood blocks or marvers or wet newspapers or a combination of all three to shape the form as you inflate it." He pointed to the two workmen who were doing just that.

Quint helped her insert the bubble of glass into the ribbed optic mold. "Now step up on the stool and blow an evenly spaced pattern into the glass."

Jorgie stepped up on the stool, her stomach quivering with excitement. This was so much fun. To think she'd gathered hot molten glass on a thin rod and now she was going to blow into the tube and inflate the glass into a vase. A miracle. She put her lips to the pipe.

"Blow, blow, hard," Quint coached.

As she blew as hard as she could, Jorgie saw the piece expanding to fit the mold. A thrill chased up her spine.

"Now, gently suck in to free the glass from the mold," he murmured, his hand on her arm. "Easy."

She sucked in and the glass popped free. The glass, ribbed from the mold, glowed yellow on the end of the blowpipe.

"Let's move it over here." He guided her to two narrow metal vertical racks with a wooden bench seat in between them, and helped her settle the blowpipe on it with the hot glass dangling free off one rack. "Crouch down on the other side of the rack and blow gently into the pipe while I help form the glass."

She squatted and blew, moving along with the rod as Quint rolled it to and fro while he took up a jack to form a constriction in the glass, creating a neck line.

Together, they turned the rod. She blew while he pulled and stretched the glass with the jack. It was as if they were performing a perfect ballet.

"Looking good." He nodded. "Next step is to finish the

shape and flatten the bottom. To do that we're going to transfer the piece onto a punty for finishing the top part."

"Punty?" She arched an eyebrow.

"It's another metal rod, shorter than a blowpipe."

"Punty, jack, glory hole. This profession is full of sexual innuendo."

"They don't call it the romance of Venice for nothing." Quint winked.

Umberto handed him a punty and Quint showed her how to transfer it from the blowpipe. Using smaller jacks, he dropped water onto the neck line of the vase and lightly tapped the blowpipe to disconnect the glass. Then he heated the lip and flared it open. Once he was finished, he knocked the piece off the punty and put it in the annealer for slow cooling.

"You did it," he said. "You made a vase."

Jorgie clapped; her hand made a muffled sound against the Kevlar glove. "This is fantastic."

"I'm so proud of you." He held her at the waist and pulled her close for a kiss. It was only then Jorgie realized her face was dewed with perspiration from the hot room.

Quint didn't seem to mind. His kiss was long and slow and sultry, and Jorgie just enjoyed.

# 10

*Sweep her off her feet*
*—Make Love Like Casanova*

QUINT BROKE THE KISS and looked into her face, felt his breath catch in his lungs. Jorgie's eyes were wide, her lips wet from his. Her cheeks were burnished a high pink.

He didn't have to look around to know the room was empty, there was only silence, except for the sound of his blood pounding through his ears. He'd promised Uberto a handsome bribe if he'd clear out the glass shop once Jorgie had finished her projects. Apparently, Uberto had successfully convinced the glassmakers to take an early lunch and leave them alone.

It was a total Casanova move and he wasn't the least bit ashamed of himself. Along with the picnic basket he'd ordered ahead of time and had delivered to the shop. He turned and spied the white wicker basket with the blue-and-white checked cloth positioned beside the door, where Umberto must have left it for him.

"Where did everyone go?" Jorgie asked.

Quint smiled at her. "I've arranged for us to have a private lunch."

"What makes you think I'd be comfortable with that?"

He tilted his head. "Are you uncomfortable, Jorgie?"

"You're a smooth operator, you know that, Quint Mason."

"Smooth as that vase you just made, Jorgie Gerard."

She returned his smile, a little reluctantly, a little hesitantly, but she did return it. She might not be a stunning beauty, but she was pretty and when she smiled, it made his heart light up in a dozen different places.

"Wanna have lunch?" He inclined his head in the direction of the picnic basket.

"Where did that come from?"

"I have my sources."

"You're trying really hard to sweep me off my feet."

"Is it working?"

"A little," she admitted.

"Come on," he said, and held out his hand.

"Where?"

"You'll see."

She allowed him to take her hand. On the way to the exit, he picked up the picnic basket and guided her through the door into a narrow corridor and up a flight of crooked stairs. At the head of the stairs was another door. He opened it and they stepped out onto the roof of the glass shop. The balmy breeze was a refreshing caress after the heat of the glass shop.

The roof was slightly sloped on the back side and when he spread out the blue-and-white checked cloth for them to sit on they couldn't see or be seen from the street below. In front of them stretched the lagoon. They saw water taxis scurrying back and forth in the distance.

"Oh," she said. "It's beautiful up here."

"The perfect place for a picnic."

"Did Gia bring you up here?" she asked.

"She did," he admitted.

"Did you make love up here?"

"We didn't." He grinned. "But I like the way you think."

Jorgie ducked her head, reached for the basket. "Whatcha got to eat?"

"I don't know. I left it up to Uberto. We'll find out together."

They dug through the basket like kids on a scavenger hunt, unearthing salami, a jar of olives, sun-dried tomatoes, a crusty loaf of bread and a thick chunk of cheese. They made quick work of the feast, washing it down with red wine Uberto had tucked inside the basket. He'd forgotten to include glasses, so they ended up passing the bottle back and forth between them.

"Um, are there any napkins?" she asked. "Instead of licking my fingers."

"Hmm, I wouldn't mind licking them for you."

She rolled her eyes at that.

"Ah, here they are at the bottom," he said, and handed her the napkins with a flourish. "Saved from having your fingers licked."

She dabbed her fingers dry and dropped the napkin back into the basket. Then she paused and slanted him a look. "The view is amazing from up here, and I just realized something."

"What's that?" he asked, the expression on her face sending his pulse jumping.

"No one can see us up here. The shop sign hides us from behind. That old olive tree shields us from the west, the building next door blocks us from the east. The only place where anyone could see us on this roof is from the water, and they'd have to be very close. We'd see them coming long before they saw us."

"What are you suggesting?" Quint asked, hoping against hope Jorgie was thinking what he was thinking.

"I'm thinking Casanova would take full advantage of an opportunity like this."

"Are you, now?" He slid closer to her. "Acrobatics might be a bit tricky on this roof. Could slip off, fall into the water."

"That's what makes it so exciting," she whispered.

"Jorgie Gerard, you little minx." Here she was issuing him a dare, a challenge, a call to adventure. Did the woman have any clue how much she aroused his interest and stirred his blood? His curiosity was provoked. His body prickled with keen urgency.

He'd never expected anything so audacious from sweet, innocent Jorgie. She reached for the snap on his jeans.

Spellbound, he stared, his jaw unhinged. Adrenaline pumped through his veins. Testosterone flooded his cock.

Quint realized then how little he really knew about her, and that thought served to send his desire spiraling even higher.

Her wicked wink sent a bolt of exquisitely excruciating lust jolting to the very center of him. He looked into her eyes and she looked into him. A heartbeat passed.

"I'm not wearing any underwear," she whispered.

His libido slammed into fifth gear.

Then her lips, stained dark pink from the wine, parted and she slipped the tip of her tongue between pearly white teeth in a gesture so erotic, he almost came right then and there.

"What do you think about that?" she asked.

His gaze locked on the V between her thighs. He could not spy a panty line beneath her white shorts. Was she really going commando or just wearing a thong? Hell, did it matter? Just the suggestion lit him up hotter than a glory hole. His mouth was dry, his stomach clenched, his brain a bundle of erotic images, all starring Jorgie.

He'd never experienced any sensation like this, and Quint had experienced a lot of sensations. Her fingers were still on the snap of his jeans, not undoing them, but not moving, either. His cock was granite. Who could have believed something this simple would feel so incredible? He could scarcely breathe, much less think.

Their gazes were still locked.

Her suddenly bold sexual confidence belied what he knew about her. She was sweet and a little shy. Or so he'd always thought. Then again, you had to watch out for the quiet ones. Still waters and all that. He had to admit she was a lot more complex than he realized and he yearned to find out just how complicated she really was.

Hungry curiosity prodded at him. Time hung suspended between them. Her hand curled around his waistband, her gaze hung on his lips, the air hung rich with the heated smell of Murano, the tile roof smooth beneath his butt.

He'd started this strange dance. He was the one who'd lured her away from the group, brought her to the Veneziani Glass Shop for a very private lesson and coaxed her up on this roof for a secluded picnic. But damn if she wasn't the one finishing it.

In the glow from the noonday sun peeping over the branches of the olive tree, he trailed his gaze from her face to her bosom, which was rising and falling rapidly as she drew in air. The red-and-white polka-dot blouse she wore molded softly to her breasts. His gaze traveled lower to her waist and beyond. The white shorts she had on snugly hugged her hips and thighs.

She undid the snap of his jeans.

His erection burgeoned against her hand.

She stroked him through the denim as she eased down his zipper. Quint felt his butt muscles contract.

Then she leaned forward and nipped his chin with her teeth. Not hard, but not so soft, either.

He swallowed back a groan.

"Handling that blowpipe got me to thinking," she said softly.

He could smell her scent and it was driving him mad. "Yeah?"

She straddled him. His pants were unsnapped, his zipper undone. She touched his shoulder with the palm of her hand and pushed him back against the roof. "I liked it."

"Uh-huh." He couldn't have formed a complete sentence if he wanted to. Damn, who was she?

She ran her tongue over her lips. "I like the feel of the pipe against my mouth. Hot and firm."

He nodded, still completely incapable of speech at this point.

Jorgie scooted down the roof until her bottom was resting on his knees. With one hand, she pushed the hem of his shirt upward, exposing a strip of his belly to the warm sun and the cool sea breeze. It was a tantalizing combo of sensations. He loved the game she was playing. The woman was amazing.

Then she reached through the open zipper and... and...Quint's eyes rolled back in his head with sheer pleasure as she freed his erection from his pants. "Jorgie." He panted, hardly breathing. "Jorgie."

"You may call me Lady Evangeline."

Ah, was that what she was playing at? He grinned. Okay, fine. He reached up to touch her, to pull her head down for another kiss, but Lady Evangeline had other ideas.

She had one hand wrapped around his stiff cock as she slowly lowered so that her tongue could touch his throbbing head. He was a goner. He was welded to the roof, unable to move. He was nothing but molten glass between her nimble lips.

Around and around she swirled that wicked little instrument of pure torture. Up and down, a tantalizing, mind-blowing blend of expert maneuvers that put any courtesan to shame. What in the hell had they been teaching her in that class?

"You are a nasty girl."

"That's right, Casanova, talk dirty to me."

He told her then, in very graphic terms, exactly what he wanted to do to her. He wanted to strip off her clothes, roll her over onto the roof and pour himself into the hot glory of her. He wanted to plunge and plunge and plunge until he'd fused her to him like glass to a blowpipe.

She increased the tempo of her strokes, nibbling and sucking, pulling him in and out of her succulent mouth, bringing him closer and closer to the edge of insanity. He lost all ability to think, to move from his spread-eagle position on that blue-and-white checked tablecloth on the roof of the glass shop. He felt the orgasm growing and growing and growing, hard and hot and unstoppable.

"Jorgie," he cried out. An invisible wall of water flooded over him. His body arched in an involuntary response. The sky above spun, clouds whizzed past him. It was a visual explosion of light, taste, scent and sound.

His toes curled. His lips curled. Hell, even his hair probably curled.

A split second later, his essence spurted into the warm

moistness of her welcoming mouth and his entire body went slack.

Jorgie angled him the most wicked Lady Evangeline smile he could imagine and delicately swallowed. Then she took the napkin from the picnic basket, dabbed at her mouth and cleaned him up. Zippered his pants. Snapped the snap.

Breathlessly, Quint reached for her, intent on pulling her to his chest and telling her how much he appreciated what she'd just done for him, how he couldn't wait to do the same thing for her.

But Lady Evangeline slipped through his fingers. She got to her feet, picked up the picnic basket and headed for the door.

"Wait, wait," he gasped, propping himself up on his elbows.

She stopped with her hand on the door, cocked her head back over her shoulder and winked at him before she disappeared down the stairs.

SEXUAL EMPOWERMENT quickened Jorgie's step.

Wow. Just wow. She could not believe what she'd actually done.

She walked down the streets of Murano, white wicker picnic basket dangling from her arm. Head held high, smiling at everyone she passed. People smiled back, waved, called out, *"Buon pomeriggio."* She'd never felt so strong, so alive, so in charge of her life. Taking the lead in a sexual liaison had given her unexpected self-confidence.

And even though she had the urge to check and see if Quint had followed, she never looked back. A sly courtesan would never have looked back. Lady Evangeline would never have looked back at Casanova. Looking back would reveal vulnerability.

"You were awesome," she whispered to herself.

Avery would be so proud of her, that she'd finally done something bold and daring and totally out of character. Even now, with the warm sun beating down on her and the creak of wicker in her ears, thinking about how she'd unzipped Quint's pants and brought him to orgasm up there on the roof caused her lips to tremble and her tongue to recall the salty masculine taste of him.

Except now, she knew it wasn't enough. She wanted more. She ached to be even bolder, even more brazen. Sexual clout, she discovered, was a very heady rush. Now she understood what Avery had been talking about all these years.

Jorgie caught a glimpse of herself in a shop window. Her hair was a wild tumble about her shoulders and she couldn't even remember when the band around her tresses had broken free. A feral expression of smug satisfaction tipped up the corners of her lips stained dark pink from wine and certain illicit activities and she found she could not stop grinning.

She simply couldn't wait to do it again.

AFTER COLLECTING his scattered thoughts and stuffing his shirt back into his waistband, Quint clattered down the stairs after Jorgie only to find himself halted by Uberto and the two other glassmakers returning from their lunch break.

"Did you see Jorgie come through here?" he asked Uberto in Italian.

"We saw her on the street," Uberto said. "She was smiling. It seems you've still got it, my friend. The charm of Casanova. Send them on their way with a smile on their faces, no?"

No. Not at all. In fact, it was the other way around. Jorgie had left him with a smile on his face. Jolted, Quint recalled no woman had ever gone off and left him after a romantic interlude. It had always been him slipping away. Leaving with a kiss and some sort of romantic gesture, but leaving all the same.

But Jorgie had left him.

A sadness unlike anything he'd ever felt before swept over him. Was this what the women felt like when he'd left them—lonely, sheepish, awkward, lost? The thought bothered him. A lot.

"Ciao," he told Uberto and headed for the door. "Thanks for letting me show her the shop and for setting up the picnic."

"Wait." Uberto stalked toward the annealer, holding him up when more than anything he longed to race after Jorgie. "The little cat piece you made for her should be cool enough to take with you. The vase she made I'll send over to your resort with tomorrow's deliveries to Venice."

Impatiently, he shifted his weight while Uberto took the cat from the annealer and boxed it up. The entire time, he kept thinking about Jorgie. He had no idea she was so sensual. You would never guess it from looking at her. She seemed so sweet and innocent with those wide blue eyes and long dark lashes and the way she dipped her head so coyly.

A shudder of desire ran through him as he recalled the feel of her lips on his cock. She was beyond anything he'd ever expected. She twisted him like a pretzel, expertly working him over. He tried to tell himself he was overstating the case. That he was so impressed simply because it had been a while since he'd been with a woman. Especially a woman that had captivated him the way she did. But deep inside, he could not deny the truth.

Everything about her spoke to something deep within

him. She struck a chord he hadn't known was there. Her sweet-yet-sexy scent, her soft voice, her ability to startle and shock him. He even liked the way she ran hot one minute and cool the next. He couldn't figure her out. He felt as if he'd been waiting his entire life to find her.

What did she think of him? That question kept him dangling, like glass from a blowpipe—hot and ready to crack. Was he just a vacation fling for her? And if so, why did that idea bother the hell out of him? He'd never minded being anyone's vacation booty call before.

He grabbed the box from Uberto and ran from the glass shop. He couldn't wait to find her, to see her again, to figure out where this was going and what it all meant. He rushed through the streets, his eyes on the lookout for a curvy brunette in a white-and-red polka-dot shirt and body-hugging white shorts.

At last, he spied her, standing with some of the other tourists from the Eros resort queuing up at the vaporetto launch. She was talking to a man and laughing.

Jealousy, sharp and quick, took a bite out of him.

He rushed up to her, even as the voice in the back of his head told him to be cool. "There you are," he said breathlessly, angling a dirty look at the guy standing too close to her.

"Hello," she said smoothly. "Have you met Ace?" She gestured toward the man. "Ace this is Quint. Quint, Ace."

He nodded curtly to the guy. Ace stuck out his hand for a handshake, but Quint ignored it and the guy finally lowered his hand to his side.

"Ace was telling me that Venice is slowly sinking into the lagoon. Isn't that a travesty?"

"Tragic," he replied. He took her by the arm. "Can we talk?"

"Why, sure." Her tone was light, as if fifteen minutes ago they hadn't been up on the roof doing what they'd been doing. "What's on your mind?"

"In private?"

"Okay."

His gut tightened and he was about to direct her away from the crowd when the vaporetto docked and everyone started climbing aboard.

"Our ride is here. Looks like that private talk will have to wait," she said, and gently removed her arm from his grasp.

Quint scowled at the boat. Nothing was going as planned. He'd intended on seducing Jorgie, not the other way around. He spotted several of his students watching him. *Quick, what would Casanova do?*

"You look so beautiful," he said, surprised at how heart-felt the words sounded in the languid air.

Her cheeks pinked and she ducked her head. "Don't toy with me, Quint. I know I'm not beautiful."

True enough, she wasn't a classic beauty, but suddenly in the reflected glow of the sun off the water, Quint saw her in the same way Da Vinci must have seen Mona Lisa and been inspired to paint her. A saucy cheekiness lurked in her startling blue eyes, buried beneath the conventions of a middle-class suburban upbringing, but it was there nonetheless. She possessed a determined set to her lips that told him come what may, Jorgie was the kind of woman you could count on.

"Oh," she said, her eyes widening in understanding. "You're playing Casanova for your students, aren't you? You want me to react like one of his conquests would?"

He opened his mouth, not sure of what he was going to say, when she reached out and took the box with the little glass cat nestled inside from his hands.

"For me?" she said loudly enough for those around them to hear. "How thoughtful." Then she leaned over and brushed her lips over his cheekbone.

That sweet kiss, that innocent kiss, that most chaste of kisses in light of what she'd just done on the rooftop of the glass shop served to unglue him more effectively than if she'd lip-locked him in a red-hot, openmouthed kiss.

JORGIE WALKED DOWN the corridor toward her room at the Eros resort, the box with the little glass cat inside clutched in her hands, her mind a mad jumble. On the vaporetto, while Quint was playing at being Casanova and she'd kissed him on the cheek, he'd had the saddest expression in his eyes. As if he were saying goodbye to an old friend he knew he'd never see again. It unsettled her in a way she could not describe. She'd never expected Quint to look sad. Honestly, she didn't know he had that much depth of emotion. To look so poignant after she'd given him a blow job.

She smiled at the memory of their rooftop rendezvous. She'd never used her sexuality to control a man before, had never really understood that she could. The courtesan classes had opened her eyes to a lot of things she'd never seen before. How she'd been holding back, shutting down her natural impulses, hiding her feminine talents.

It was long past time she took responsibility for her sexuality, and Quint was the instrument of her rebirth. She knew she didn't have to worry about hurting him. He'd made it clear enough he wasn't a long-term relationship kind of guy. This was all about fun and learning about what she needed in bed. It was a lesson she should have learned long ago.

She'd been born with a cautious, reliable nature. As a

child she'd valued tranquility and courted the status quo, but
through knowing Avery, she'd learned that sometimes you
had to shake things up to get noticed. That's why she was
here. To shake things up. Get noticed. Take charge of her life.

Still, a part of her was scared. Afraid of getting hurt, terrified of ending up with egg on her face.

One of Avery's favorite sayings popped into her head.
*You gotta break some eggs to make an omelet.* Well, if
Avery knew what she'd done today, she'd have applauded.

So what next? Where did she take things from here?

*Call Avery, she'll know what to do.*

She dug her phone from her purse. "Guess what I did,"
she said as soon as Avery answered. Then she launched
into detail about her adventure on Murano.

"That's wonderful!" Avery said, laughing. "Good for
you."

"I never thought I'd be saying this, but thank you for
giving me the slip at the airport."

"I told you it was for your own good."

"Listen, I'm calling because I need your advice. I don't
know what to do next."

"Hey," Avery said, "I'm not the best person to be giving
love advice."

"I'm not looking for love advice. Love is the last thing
on my mind. I want to make this the best sexual experience of not just my life, but his, too."

"I'm pretty well batting zero on that score, as well."
Avery sighed.

Jorgie straightened at the sound of frustration in her
friend's voice. "What's wrong?"

"Let's talk about you," Avery said.

Because she really wanted to talk about what was going
on between her and Quint, Jorgie let her friend off the

hook. "I want to tease him. String him along. I want to make him think he has absolutely no chance of ever getting me all the way into his bed, and then just when he's crazy with desire I'm going to lower the boom and give him the best sex he's ever had."

"Oooh, wicked. I like it."

"So what should my next move be?"

"Does Eros have anything planned for tomorrow night? I know our resort has nightly mixers. Although Jake hasn't been to a single one of them," Avery muttered under her breath.

"Who's Jake?"

"Never mind. This conversation is about you and Quint. About that mixer…"

"Um, hang on." Jorgie got up off the bed and went to pick up the flyer that housekeeping left on the bureau every morning. "There's a carnival mask-making competition for couples and you compete against other teams to create the most erotic mask."

"That sounds perfect. Not only are you involved in a sexy endeavor but you'll be working as a team in competition with others. Men love competing and doing activities with you. It's how guys bond."

Avery made it sound so easy. "Okay," she said. "I'll give it a try."

"Let me know how it goes."

"And you keep me posted about Jake."

"Yeah, right, that's going nowhere. Anyway, I hope you have better luck with Quint. Talk to you later."

"Bye."

Jorgie switched off her phone, excitement pounding her heart. The more she thought about the erotic mask-making contest, the better she liked the idea. Taking a deep breath to calm her jangled nerves, she then hurriedly called Quint before she lost her courage.

"'Lo," he answered breezily.

"Quint, this is Jorgie. I want to enter the mask-making contest tomorrow night, but I need a partner. Are you interested?"

"You and me kicking everyone else's ass?" He laughed. "I'm so there."

"See you in the salon at seven, then."

"I'll be counting the seconds," he said.

*Me, too.*

# *11*

*The most captivating film femme fatale can seduce
a man with nothing more than her eyes*
*—Make Love Like a Movie Star*

WHILE JORGIE was getting charged up about the mask-making competition, in Los Angles Avery was trying to figure out why all her attempts to seduce Jake Stewart had failed.

The filming of her movie had to be cancelled when half the crew ended up suffering from food poisoning. She was left with too much time on her hands. She strolled the grounds of the resort, got a massage at the spa and talked to Jorgie, but it seemed nothing could assuage her restlessness. She was unaccustomed to having men resist her advances.

When she got back to her room, she glanced to the open blinds of the window and she could see straight into the window next door. Jake's blinds were open, as well.

Was he there? Watching?

She squinted and thought she could see movement inside the other bungalow. Or was it just a shadow from the ruffle of curtains in the breeze?

Her breath quickened and she felt a mesmeric force pulling her closer to the window. She was ready to take this thing to the next level. She was determined to get his attention.

"If you're over there, dude, I'm going to give you the show of your life," she muttered under her breath. "And even if you're not, one way or the other, I'm going to get an orgasm out of the deal. I've been seven months without sex and that's seven months too long."

Positioning herself squarely in front of the window, she grabbed the hem of her cropped T-shirt and slowly peeled it over her head. Then she shimmied from her pants, turning as she did so just in case Jake was watching. She wanted him to get a complete 360 of what he was missing.

When she'd finished, she stretched out across the foot of the bed, positioning herself so that her hair dangled over the edge, spreading out like a purple fan. She didn't care if Jake was watching her or not. She was having a good time all by herself. Why did she care if he hadn't responded to her nightly stripteases? There were certainly a lot more fish in the sea.

She touched herself, lightly trailing her fingers over her bare stomach and thought of the way he'd smelled that day on the soundstage when he pulled her into his arms for a kiss. She could easily recall his clean, masculine scent. Closing her eyes, she luxuriated in the moment.

Against the backs of her eyelids, she saw Jake, the dark-eyed man she'd been unable to sway. Desire for him tugged at her.

"Avery," she imagined him whispering her name in his sultry, velvet-smooth voice that sent shivers down her spine.

Her heart slammed against her rib cage at the thought of Jake settling onto the soft bed beside her. Her nipples hardened and her breasts swelled. Heat pooled deep inside her.

She envisioned his hands, broad and flat, gently caressing her skin, skimming down her throat, cupping her naked breasts, moving lower, circling her navel, teasing her mercilessly.

Mewling softly, Avery used her index finger and her thumb to lightly pinch one of her straining nipples, pantomiming what she wished Jake would do to her.

She sank her teeth into her bottom lip, eyes still closed, exploring her own body with eager fingertips. This was good. A release of sexual tension.

Her hot spine stiffened against the pillow-top mattress. Hungrily, Avery stroked the naked flesh between her thighs and all her pent-up insecurities escaped on a shattered sigh.

"Jake."

Just thinking about him and the kiss he'd given—never mind that it had been a screen kiss—made Avery feel achy and wet and hot. She traced her fingertips over tender skin, across the silky folds, skimming along the satiny moisture oozing slowly from her swollen inner core.

"Jake," she murmured again.

She pictured him with her—his caress, his hand, kneading the delicate bud, dangling her on the edge of pleasure. She envisioned his mouth covering hers, his tongue nibbling, tasting, exploring. Her heart raced and her mind spun out of control.

His hand dipped between her legs, caressing, rubbing her swollen sex. He drew small circles against her inner thigh with his thumb.

Her fingers moved in time with the fantasy. She was in it all the way now. No turning back. Her orgasm was so close, beckoning her onward.

*Come.*

Faster and faster her fingers strummed, adding more pressure, taking her more quickly toward her goal. Release. Relief.

"Jake, Jake, Jake," she cried, thrashing about in the covers. She was burning up from the inside out.

In her mind's eye she saw him, looking at her with ravenous eyes, poised over her. His manhood, thick and swollen with desire, pushing against her wet flesh, sliding into her innermost cave. Dilating her, taking her, claiming her.

The orgasm ripped through her in a sudden rush. Legs stiffening, Avery arched her hips and cried out, gratification humming though her body.

She came hard, but it wasn't adequate. She wanted more. Her release, no matter how good, was steeped with loneliness. The fantasy did not compare to reality. She wanted more.

She wanted *him*.

While Avery lay writhing in sexual ecstasy, Jake stood in the shadows of his room, his fingernails digging into his palms. Twin impulses of aggravation and desire battled inside him. The woman was a dangerous tease. If he was a smart man, he would turn and walk right out of the room. Instead, he stayed rooted to the spot.

Clearly, he was not a smart man.

The truth was, she'd gotten to him, slipped under his radar. Jake was stunned to discover how little self-control he really possessed when it came to this woman.

It scared him.

He'd been wound tighter than wire on a spool ever since he'd kissed her on the movie set. There was no denying it. The kiss had obviously fired her up, too.

And it took every ounce of masculine strength he possessed not to march into her bungalow, climb onto that bed with her and make love to her all night long.

Jake clenched his jaw. He couldn't, he wouldn't act on impulse. He was a controlled man, but his erection was so hard he could barely draw in air. Dammit, he wanted her.

She'd done this to him. Made him desire her in a way he'd never desired another.

He tried to think of how lust had gotten him into trouble before. But this felt like so much more than just lust. This felt like…*destiny*.

Avery turned him on and turned him inside out.

His hand strayed to the zipper of his jeans, his fingers fumbled as his breath came hard and fast. He imagined it was Avery provoking him, stroking him.

Her fantasy touch caused every nerve ending in his body to jolt with awareness as he recalled the feel of her soft lips, the sweet taste of her tongue. He visualized her long, silken curls tickling his bare skin. He saw her full, pink lips tip up in a beguiling grin.

Daydream mingled with memory as his imagination escalated the scenario playing out in his head. His shaft throbbed. His pulse raced. His brain hung on one thought and one thought only.

*Avery.*

*Stop, stop. You've got to stop this.*

But it was too late for that. His self-control was shot. He was lost. Overcome.

He stripped off his jeans and touched himself. His rhythm was frantic, desperate. He felt in equal parts embarrassment and inevitability. He had to do something to alleviate the weighted need that had settled in.

*Just get it over with. Quick. Empty out the testosterone. Get your brain back.*

He closed his eyes, took in a deep breath and then did what he had to do to reclaim his sanity.

*Avery.*

A groan, half pleasure, half despair, slipped past his lips. How he wished she was the one doing this to him.

His blood pounded through his veins. There was no stopping now. What had the woman reduced him to?

And then the orgasm was upon him.

*Avery.*

Clenching his jaw, he shuddered as ribbons of milky heat shot up and spilled over his fist.

When it was over and he'd cleaned himself up, he collapsed onto the bed. In the bungalow across the way, Avery lay motionless on her bed, sated, as was he.

He could hear his own heartbeat, imagine the black, mysterious shadows of her darkened room. He inhaled it—the night—smelling thickly of his unsatisfying sexual release.

Dammit, he was here to do a job and he couldn't concentrate. He'd never been so distracted. He was supposed to be catching a saboteur; instead, fate had delivered him an unexpected complication.

*Avery.*

Jake draped a forearm over his eyes. He had to find a way to get his brain back. Now.

And that's when the cell phone went off that had the special ring tone he'd installed for when his boss, Dougal Lockhart, called.

Something was up.

HAD HE SEEN HER? Had he watched? Avery couldn't stand not knowing. It made her feel irritable and antsy in spite of the orgasm she'd just given herself.

She thought about him in the bungalow across the way,

that dark-haired, dark-eyed enigma of a man. Perspiration dewed her forehead. Her blood flowed thick with desire for him. She was already horny again.

So, had he seen her or not? Had he watched her and touched himself as had been her intent? Or had he gone to bed, oblivious of her erotic peep show? Or…and she hated to think this…had he been disgusted by her behavior and shut the blinds.

At that idea a hot flush of humiliation burned her throat. Avery reached up to touch her lips. The kiss he'd given her on the set told her he'd been anything but disgusted, and yet she couldn't help feeling insecure. She really liked this guy. More than she'd liked anyone in a long time.

*Hell, you barely know him.*

That might be true, but she couldn't help the way she felt when she was around him—alive and yet calmed, stimulated and yet soothed, energized and yet balanced. On her own, she was a spinning top. If she ever stopped, she'd fall over. Hence she never stopped. But around Jake, she had the strongest urge to slow down and savor each second like a sinful bite of perfect chocolate cake.

So had Jake seen her and reacted, or not?

Anxiously, she swung her legs over the side of bed, pulling the sheet with her and wrapping it around her naked body. Then, holding her breath, she padded to the window and peeked across the way.

His blinds were still open.

Her heart jumped and she moved closer, squinting in the darkness.

She spied him then, pacing the bedroom of the bungalow across the way. Buck naked, cell phone pressed to his ear.

Air leaked slowly from her lungs as she took him in.

The man was beyond magnificent. The reality surpassed any fantasy she'd dreamed up about him.

His body was a work of art, no two ways about it. Had any life-form on earth had a greater impact on her? *Gorgeous* was not a good word. *Handsome* didn't begin to cover it. *Exquisite* lacked the necessary wonderment she felt at gazing upon this most masculine of males.

Lean, but muscular. Honed and toned and tanned. Impressive pectorals, abs that put washboards to shame. A sprinkling of dark hair trailed from his upper chest down toward his abdomen. Thick, ropey veins crisscrossed his torso, a testament to a good cardiovascular system. Her fingers itched to stroke him. She wished she was closer, could see more, could trace those lines of muscles and veins, sinew and bones down, down, down to the part of him that was uniquely and utter male.

Talk about well endowed! Avery licked her lips and moaned softly. Wonder what he tasted like? Earthy and rich and virile, no doubt. Salty and tangy and delicious.

She knew at once how special this moment was. The first time she saw her lover naked. She drank him in, committed every minute detail to memory.

*He's not your lover.*

Maybe not yet, but one way or the other, Avery was determined to make this man hers.

"THE INCIDENT of food poisoning at the resort was not accidental," Dougal Lockhart told Jake over the phone.

"How do you know?" Jake asked.

He paced the length of the bedroom. The night air drifting in through the open window was warm against his skin. His nerves were stretched as taut as piano wire. He splayed a hand to the nape of his neck, dug his fingers into tense muscles. He was trying to listen to his boss, but his mind was on Avery.

"Taylor just got another threatening letter," Dougal said. "I'm forwarding it to you. But he's claiming responsibility for the food poisoning."

Guilt tore at his gut. This had happened on his watch. While he'd been busy thinking about Avery and doing things he shouldn't have been doing, someone had been tampering with the resort's food supply. "You're sure it's a he?"

"Not certain, no. Just using the pronoun for convenience. It could just as easily be a woman."

"And Taylor honestly has no idea who could be doing this to her?" he asked.

"She's in a position of power, and there's some people who've made value judgments against what she does for a living."

"Yeah, but having an opposing opinion is one thing, taking it to this kind of extreme is another."

"I agree."

"Have we put the people closest to her under a microscope? Turned over every rock. Looked in every nook and cranny."

"Been there," Dougal said, "repeatedly. Taylor doesn't have much family. Her husband, Daniel, who's my best friend. That's about it."

"No parents, siblings?"

"No siblings. Mother died when she was a kid. Father passed away a few years ago and left her the airline. No aunts or uncles, cousins are distant. She does have godparents."

"What about them? Could they be responsible? So often this kind of thing goes back to loved ones."

"Her godfather is General Charles Miller."

"Oh," Jake said. "Well, it's not like he'd do something like this."

"No." Dougal's sigh reverberated over the airwaves. "I'm beginning to think we're never going to catch this saboteur."

"What's the saboteur hoping to gain from this?" Jake asked. "What's his or her motive? Revenge for something? They're not trying to extort money from her, right? So financial gain is out of the picture."

"Not so far. From the gist of the threatening letters, I get the feeling the perpetrator wants to scare her into closing down her operation. Some wacko who feels sexy fantasy resorts are immoral."

"Ah, the moral crusader," Jake said. "They're often the most difficult culprits to get a bead on."

"I know. We've looked at some of the people who protested her resorts when she first opened them, but came up empty-handed."

"It's frustrating."

"Yeah. Listen, just be extra vigilant. I hate to fail, and I've promised Taylor we're going to catch this guy."

"Will do. Anything going on at any of the other three resorts?"

"Not so far. Looks like all the action is in L.A. Taylor is sending out a team of investigators to see if they can find out how the food got tainted, but we want to keep it on the Q.T. Don't want to alarm the guests."

"Gotcha."

"Remember, until proven otherwise, everyone is a suspect," Dougal reminded him.

"I always assume that." Jake's gaze drifted to the window. That meant Avery was a suspect, whether he liked it or not. Could she be behind this? Was that why she was coming on so strong? She'd figured out who he really was and she was toying with him?

Immediately, he dismissed that thought. He didn't know her well, but his instincts told him Avery was totally aboveboard. From what he could tell, the woman hid nothing. But he couldn't afford to make any assumptions. Until the saboteur was located, he had to be on guard.

And then after that?

"Let me know if anything out of the ordinary happens. If the perp hadn't taken credit for the food poisoning, we would have put it off as an accident."

"Will do."

"Good night."

"Night." Jake hit the end button and tossed his cell phone on the dresser. His gaze fell on the gauzy curtains blowing in the breeze. Tension knotted his stomach. What was Avery doing over there? Had she gone to bed? Was she still awake?

He shouldn't care. He shouldn't be thinking like this, but he couldn't seem to help himself. Like a moth to a flame, he felt drawn toward the window.

Naked as the day he was born, he stepped in front of it, never expecting to find her standing at her window staring straight at him.

Their eyes met, gazes locked.

His breath stilled in his lungs and he felt an overwhelming urge to exit through the window, stalk the few short feet between them and climb into her bedroom.

Avery's sweet perfect mouth formed a startled O.

Jake's cock hardened instantly.

Avery raised a hand and for one stupid moment he

thought she was waving, beckoning him over. He actually stepped closer to the window.

And then she snapped closed the blinds.

Leaving Jake standing there feeling like a fool.

# *12*

*To truly bond with a man, engage him in competition*
*—Make Love Like a Courtesan*

A WIDE ARRAY of mask-making supplies greeted Jorgie when she walked into the room where the event was being held. Preformed, white plaster masks had been laid out on a long folding table. There were three different kinds—the simple eye mask, called a *columbina;* the full-face mask, known as a *volto;* and the suggestive, long-nosed mask, dubbed a *nasone* in Italian.

The art supplies lay on another table adjacent to the one with the masks. A generous assortment of colorful feathers sprawled across one section—ostrich, peacock, turkey. There were a myriad of ribbons in every hue of the rainbow and braided trim of rich fabrics, along with Swarovski crystals, beads, buttons and felt. The tools included scissors, X-Acto knives, primer paint, craft glue, heat guns and sandpaper.

Jorgie reached for the long proboscis of a nose mask.

"Remind you of anything?" Quint's low deep voice caused her to jump and her face to heat.

"You are such a perv," she said, battling against the flush of guilty pleasure rising up her neck. Because, let's face it, the noses on the nasone masks looked unsettlingly like dangling male appendages.

"Is that the mask you're going to pick?" he asked.

She clasped her hands behind her back. "No, of course not."

"You going with the full mask, then? Or the coquettish *columbina?*"

"Since we're a team I thought we'd choose together."

"Casanova favored the *nasone.*"

"What a shocker, but you can stop lobbying for the *nasone.* We're not going for the penis mask."

"Jorgie!" Quint chuckled. "I'm shocked."

"That I know what a penis is?"

"That you would say the word in public." He looked over his shoulder at the other participants filing into the room.

"Yeah, well, it's what everyone is thinking."

"Your boldness surprises me."

"I've learned a lot lately."

"Like what?"

"If you let the threat of embarrassment stop you from doing things you'll spend your life on the sidelines. Let's go with the full-face mask." She snatched one off the table and tucked it under her arm.

"Okay," he said, still laughing, and followed her as she moved on over to the art supplies. Several minutes later, they found a workstation and spread out their equipment as Maggie Cantrell explained the specifics of mask-making.

"At the end of this workshop," she said, "two Venetian artists who specialize in masks will serve as judges. The winner of the competition gets to take out one of the villa's boats for a private lunch on one of the nearby islands."

That brought noises of enthusiasm from the group.

"Ready, set, get to making your masks," Maggie encouraged.

The steps for mask-making were written on a large eraser board positioned at the front of the room, and Maggie put on a video to play featuring a Venetian artisan speaking heavily accented English.

Twenty minutes later, they were elbow-deep in hot glue and sequins and shiny glass beads. They were laughing and joking and working as a team. Amazing, how much fun they were having doing something as simple as making masks. She hadn't played like this since she was a kid.

"Does your face always light up like sunshine when you're relaxed?"

"I don't know," she said. "I guess I don't relax much."

"Your boyfriend didn't do fun stuff like this with you?"

"Are you kidding? Brian was afraid of looking ridiculous."

"You mean he would never do this?" Quint pulled a comical expression with crossed eyes that had her giggling.

"Never."

"Sounds like a dullard."

"I was just as dull." Jorgie told him about being called conventional.

"Nah, you weren't dull. He inhibited you. Why were you with him?"

Jorgie paused, pondering the question.

Quint raised an index finger that had a shiny crimson button glued to it and he waggled it at her, making her giggle again. "Unless it's too painful to talk about, in which case you can tell me to mind my nosy business."

"You know," she said, "I haven't thought about him

once since I got here. I guess I wasn't as invested in him as I believed."

"He wasn't right for you."

"How do you know? You never met the guy."

Quint shrugged. "When was the last time you laughed this hard?"

Ages and ages, and when she did laugh this hard, it was because of Avery. In fact, she couldn't think of a single time Brian had ever made her laugh.

"There's more to life than laughter," she said, feeling a little defensive.

"Yeah, but laughter makes life worth living." Quint winked. He leaned over for the hot glue gun sitting on the table beside her. His elbow brushed against her, and she knew it wasn't accidental. "Jorgie?"

"Yes?"

"This is me and you, right? No Casanova, no Lady Evangeline?"

He peeled the button off his index finger and for one lightning-quick second she saw honest emotion in his eyes, but he quickly looked away.

Her own heart moved, beat faster in response. "Um, could you hand me that spool of aqua ribbon?"

He passed her the ribbon.

She took it from him, pretending to concentrate intensely on the mask so she wouldn't have to answer his question. She dipped her head and a hank of hair fell across her face. Irritated, she pushed it behind her ears. "Dumb hair."

"What do you mean?" Quint asked. "Your hair is beautiful."

"No, it's not. It's blah brown."

"It's the color of pecan pie." He was peering at her as if he loved pecan pie, and he was standing so close she could smell his darkly sexy Quint scent. A shiver swept through her in spite of the warm evening.

"How about peacock feathers?" she asked, picking up one long, lovely plume. "Or should we go with ostrich? It's fuzzier, but the peacock is more dramatic." She held up both to compare. "What are we going for here? Tactile or visual?"

"Visual is always good, but there's nothing like touching." He made grabby motions with his fingertips.

"So the ostrich?"

"Your mask, your call."

"You don't like rocking the boat, do you?"

He smiled, shrugged. "I'm easy to get along with."

"Doesn't that make you sort of superficial?"

One eyebrow cocked up. "You're saying I'm shallow?"

"I'm saying you skim through life."

"What's wrong with that?" he asked. "It's easier."

"You keep going whichever way the wind blows and you'll end up far from where you really want to be," she predicted.

"What if I want to be where the wind blows?"

"Do you really?" she asked.

He lounged back in the chair, studied her with heavily lidded eyes. "I don't know. Stop making me think."

"Well…" she said, using the heat gun to glue the ostrich feather to the mask. "What are you hanging around me for if I strain your brain?"

"You invited me to this, remember?"

"That's because I thought you'd have some creative input. Apparently, I was wrong."

He touched her hand. Their eyes met. He shook his head. "Go with the peacock feather. It's got more flash."

She smiled, put down the ostrich plume, took the peacock feather he passed her. "Thank you. That's all I really wanted."

Quint scooped up a handful of Swarovski crystals and canted his head, watching her glue the peacock feather to the mask with a speculative gleam in his eyes. He bounced the crystals lightly in his palm, rolled them back and forth between his long fingers. His nails were clipped short, his cuticles trimmed, and there were calluses on his fingertips. Elegant hands, but masculine, as well. A paradox. Here she found a complexity that belied his casual, surface demeanor. The crystals reflected the light in his flat, broad palm.

She couldn't help being mesmerized. She could almost feel his fingers on her skin. Instantly, her body grew warm and moist, and her pulse skittered.

"Just like you wanted me to kiss you at Miley Kinslow's birthday party?"

The question ripped her gaze off his hands and onto his face. "I did not," she declared hotly.

Mischief danced in his dark eyes. "Liar. I saw you bumping the bottle with your toe trying to aim at me instead of Marty Guzman."

"You remember that?"

"I do."

"How do you remember something like that?"

"Other than the fact that you and your friend Avery kept ogling me and giggling."

"We did not."

"You did too. Come on, admit it. You were hot for me even then." He leveled her a smug grin.

Jorgie crinkled her nose at him. "I refuse to flatter your ego."

"You had a crush on me," he challenged.

"Ah, the folly of youth."

"Is that a yes? Are you admitting to a mad crush on me?"

"Are you going to help with this project or just sit there smirking?" she asked.

"The last part."

"Wrong." She pushed the scissors toward him. "Start cutting the felt."

"Slave driver."

"Slacker."

"This is fun." He beamed.

She snorted, but grinned and picked up a braided royal blue and purple ribbon. It was fun. "What do you think?"

"Matches the color of your eyes. We gotta use it."

He cut and she glued. Fifteen minutes later, they were done. Jorgie held it up to her face. "What do you think?"

His eyes took on a look she could not describe—part awe, part desire, part amusement. "I think you're amazing," he said. "And I should have kissed you at Miley Kinslow's birthday party, whether the bottle pointed at me or not."

That drew her up short, and she was glad she had the mask over her face to hide the blush creeping up her cheeks.

"I'm thinking I'd kiss you right now if we weren't surrounded by a roomful of mask-making dweebs and Maggie Cantrell wasn't glaring at us."

"She's glaring at us?" Jorgie swung around.

"Made you look." He chuckled. "You are so easy. Why are you so afraid of the disapproval of others?"

"Who says I'm afraid of the disapproval of others?" she asked, laying the mask down on the table and reaching for the elastic to make the strap for holding it in place.

"Come on, Jorgie, you're so busy being a good girl, you don't even know *what* you want."

"Said the man who goes whichever way the wind blows."

"We're quite a pair, huh? You don't know what you want and I don't know where I *want* to be." His gaze honed in on her lips, then slowly eased over her chin to her throat, sliding on down to her breasts. A sweet shiver of anticipation ran through her. Instantly, her nipples hardened. Traitors.

"The judges are here," Maggie Cantrell announced, derailing their conversation. "You have a few minutes to finish up before the judging begins."

"You think we stand a chance at winning?" Jorgie asked, putting the finishing touches on the mask. She placed a shiny gold button to cover the base of the feathers.

He nodded. "Oh, yeah."

"You're that confident?"

"No one has your flair with feathers, felt and glue. Take a look around," Quint said.

The button slipped off. "Darn it," she muttered.

"Here." He leaned over her shoulder. "Let me help you with that." His breath was warm on her skin. He smelled so good. Jorgie struggled to ignore the heat flaring through her.

His arms reached past her shoulders. She was trapped with him over her, around her. He was doing this on purpose. She knew it. A Casanova move. If some of his students weren't in the room watching, she might have told him to step off.

Actually, she was loving this. That was the trouble. All these fun and games had to end sometime.

He placed a huge dollop of hot glue on the mask and mashed the button into place. It held. Stupid button. "There you go."

Maggie Cantrell clapped for attention. "Everyone bring your completed masks to the front of the room."

Two minutes later, with the masks arranged and the judges circling the table, Quint took her hand in his. "Nervous?"

"Strangely enough, yes. Why would I be nervous over a silly mask contest?"

His sexy gaze raked over her. "Because you like to win."

She smiled back. "So do you."

"And because you want that prize of spending the day with me on a deserted island."

"Egotist," she accused, poking him playfully in the ribs with her elbow.

The judges picked up the masks and inspected them closely, as if they were taking this contest way too seriously. They whispered to each other, made notes on a pad. Finally they passed their evaluations to Maggie.

"And the winner is…"

Jorgie bit down on her bottom lip. Quint squeezed her hand.

Maggie picked up their mask. "Full-face peacock blue, created by Quint Mason and Jorgie Gerard."

"We won!" she shouted, and jumped into Quint's waiting arms.

In that singular moment of triumph all the lights went off, bathing the room in total darkness.

Several people gasped simultaneously. Jorgie gave a little "Eek" of surprise. People began murmuring and bumping around.

"It's all right, everyone," Quint called out. "The generators will kick on any moment. Just stay where you are. You don't want to trip over something and hurt yourselves in the dark."

She couldn't see anything. But she could feel the

hardness of Quint's honed chest beneath her fingers and she trembled, not with fear, but with something just as elemental.

"I'm here," he murmured in her ear. He tightened his strong, masculine arms around her, pulled her closer.

It was as if they were standing in the synapse of time, the world stretching out weirdly into nothingness. She could feel his steady heart thumping beneath his chest. In that instant, she felt safer than she'd ever felt in her life. Quint cupped his palm at the nape of her neck, and then tilted her head upward to calm her mouth with a kiss. His lips were both hot and tender.

She couldn't help but wonder if he'd somehow arranged for the lights to be doused so that he could do this to her in the dark, in a crowded room. She could hear people shifting around them, breathing and swaying, murmuring and waiting.

Jorgie was not expecting the shocking thrill of sexual excitement that sped over her nerve endings. She felt as if everything had been switched into slow motion.

It was almost as if he could read her mind. As if their hearts were beating to the same timpani. As if his breath was hers and hers his. It was the most bizarre thing she'd ever experienced.

Something about him arrested her. Something about his calm-in-the-storm aura filled her with a strong sense of déjà vu. She'd never felt such a compelling mental connection to any man in her life and yet it seemed so familiar, so right. Deep inside her, something monumental stirred. Something long buried. Something hoped for and dreamed of, but never acknowledged.

*Soul mate.*

All the caution and hesitation that had defined her life

to this point vanished, and for the first time since birth, she was freed from all restrictions, all limitations.

This was no mere flirtation. This was no simple tease. This was no ordinary male-female reaction.

Her skin tingled as the warmth of his breath feathered the minute hairs on her cheek. Her heart swelled. The rough material of his jacket lightly scratched her bare arm. His masculine scent soothed her.

He was as hard and firm as she was soft and pliable. Their mouths were frantic hunger. Her trembling increased.

"Jorgie," he murmured, breaking their kiss. "I've got you. You're all right."

His voice was thick and husky. He sounded the way red wine smelled. She found herself thinking dizzily—*cabernet, pinot noir, Syrah, merlot.* Musky and smoky, with an undercurrent of plump, tart, red sweet cherries and savory, juice-laden blackberries. You could get drunk on a voice like that.

On a man like this.

He held her in place, not moving, even as those around them crashed into things, cursing and complaining. She'd never thought of Quint as steady or reliable, but here, he was a rock. Gibraltar. Atlas. Strong, present, unmoving. Who knew he had such depth inside him?

She heard Maggie Cantrell urging everyone to stay still and remain calm, reiterating what Quint had said earlier, promising that the backup generator would kick on momentarily. But Jorgie wanted to hear *him* speak again.

She curled her fingers around his wrist and whispered provocatively. "I'm scared."

"Nothing to be afraid of." His tone was low, measured, controlled. "You're safe with me."

His quiet, deliberate words inspired her. Where was the chatty, teasing Quint? How come he was so different in the dark?

Jorgie felt the heat of his hand at her waist, the pressure of his hip resting against her pelvis. She was disoriented, lost.

Sounds were either too distant or too close, smells too sharp or too muted. The peppermint taste of him on her tongue, too sweet and too intense. The texture of his nubby jacket beneath her fingers, too authentic and yet, at the same time, too surreal.

She forgot about the mask-making competition. And forgot they weren't alone in the room. She forgot about everything except the feel of Quint's virile arms around her and the echo of his sexy voice in her ears.

She was lost in time. Lost in the moment. Lost in the dark. It was the most erotic sensation she'd experienced since their afternoon at the glass shop. The pulse in her neck kicked.

Then the lights flickered back on. The air conditioner returned to life with a stuttering hum. People applauded. And Jorgie realized something monumental. No matter how hard she tried not to, she was falling in love with Quint Mason.

QUINT ESCORTED JORGIE back to her room. The place was in a hubbub over the blackout. People were wandering through the lobby talking about what they'd been doing when the lights went out. Others were at the front desk complaining. The resort manager was running around soothing ruffled feathers by offering free nightcaps to anyone who felt they'd been inconvenienced by the loss of electricity.

Jorgie carried the mask with her like a prizefighter clutching his trophy. They lingered in the doorway of her room. From the look in her eyes he could tell she would have let him spend the night if he'd just asked, but he had work to do. He suspected that the power outage had been intentional and he was anxious to speak with the head of security, Frank Lavoy. Quint had to make do with a quick kiss.

"That was some evening," she said.

"Yeah."

"Too bad it has to end." She slanted him a come-hither look.

"On the bright side, tomorrow we've got our own private picnic."

"The bright side," she echoed.

He left her standing in the doorway, a puzzled expression on her face. No doubt she was wondering what had happened to his Casanova moves. Good. It wouldn't hurt her to wonder about him. It would up the sexual tension. Smiling at that thought, he hurried down the hall.

A few minutes later, he found Frank in a discussion with the men from the electric company. They confirmed his suspicions. The fuses had been intentionally tampered with. No way could it have been accidental or caused by bad weather.

Taylor Milton's saboteur had struck again.

# 13

*There's nothing sexier than a hint of danger*
*—Make Love Like Casanova*

QUINT DIDN'T get much sleep. For one thing, he was up half the night—calling Dougal to tell him what had happened, dusting the electrical boxes for fingerprints, going over the details of what had happened with Frank. They'd discovered that the fingerprints on the fuse box belonged only to the maintenance staff. Either those men were involved or the person who'd tampered with the box had worn gloves. And the rest of the night, he slept fitfully, his mind conjuring up dreams of he and Jorgie doing erotic things together.

"We've got another problem," Dougal said.

"What's up?"

"We had an incident at Jake's resort in Hollywood."

"What happened?"

Dougal told him about the food poisoning and the letter Taylor had received.

"Are you saying we have two saboteurs?"

"Looks like it."

"Or one saboteur who's hiring people to do his dirty work."

"That, too."

"What does your gut tell you?"

"We're being played for fools," Dougal growled.

"Yeah."

"Interview the maintenance staff. Let me know what you find."

"Will do."

Quint then spent the first part of the morning doing just that. He interviewed the staff, but came across nothing suspicious in their answers. He called Dougal back to update him.

Because it was Saturday, there was no Casanova class to teach. Most of the guests had left the villa for excursions, so the lobby was empty when he finished up his questioning of the staff. All except for one person.

Jorgie stood by the concierge stand, a big wicker basket draped on her arm, a wide smile on her face. She wore the sexiest pink-and-white sundress that made him think of cotton candy. He loved cotton candy. Her shoulders were bare, save for the tiny little straps of her dress. Her glossy brown hair fell to her shoulders like a silky dark curtain. She looked gorgeous. Stimulating. Tempting. Beautiful.

"Are you ready for our date?" she asked perkily.

Date. Um, yeah. He shouldn't be going on one. Not with a saboteur on the property. But he hated to disappoint Jorgie. Dougal trusted Frank, and they'd be back by mid-afternoon at the latest. Besides, most of the guests would be gone for the day.

"Hang on, Jorgie. I have a phone call to make." He walked off to one side and called Frank to tell him he'd be away for a few hours and to contact Dougal directly if needed. He snapped his phone closed and noticed Joe Vincent was sitting at the entrance to the Internet café, studying him with an appraising gaze. Joe gave him a wink and the "thumbs up" sign. Quint nodded at his student, then walked back to Jorgie. "Ready."

The concierge gave them the keys to the small motorboat moored outside the hotel and a map with detailed instructions on how to get to the island.

"You know how to drive a boat?" Jorgie asked.

He cocked her a knowing grin.

"Oh, I forgot. You're Mr. Charming. Of course you know how to drive a boat."

He got into the boat first, took the picnic basket from her, then reached out a hand to help her in. "And a sailboat and a race car and I can fly a plane and skydive and mountain climb and…"

"Okay, I get it. You're worldly and accomplished. But humble?" She pulled a disapproving face. "Not so much."

"I never saw any reason to hide my light under a bushel, Jorgie, and neither should you." He untied the boat from the dock and then started the engine. He sat down across from her and carefully guided the little craft through the narrow waterway leading to the Grand Canal.

Forty minutes later, after scooting through the heavy boat traffic of Venice, they were in the lagoon heading for the small, uninhabited island.

"It says here in the guidebook that the island is haunted," Jorgie read.

"Just stuff to tease the tourists."

"I don't know. It says the island was once a penal colony."

Quint made spooky noises. "Are you afraid of ghosts?"

"No, of course not. But it sounds eerie, like Alcatraz."

"Don't worry, I'll protect you," he said gallantly.

She snorted.

"What? You don't think I could protect you?"

"You're probably the one I'll be needing protection from."

"There may be other tourists there." He laughed. "If you're worried about your virtue."

But he was wrong. When they reached the island there was no one else in sight. They ran aground on the sandy beach and when Quint looked back after tying up the boat, he realized they could no longer see Venice from this vantage point.

Suddenly the wind whipped up, sprinkling them with water spray. This time, Jorgie made spooky noises. "We're all alone."

"That's not a bad thing." He winked.

"Depends on your point of view."

"What do you mean?"

"Depends on if you're Little Red Riding Hood or the Big Bad Wolf."

He took the picnic basket from her. "You know, I always thought the Big Bad Wolf got a bad rap. He just needed a good spin doctor."

Jorgie scoffed. "You would."

"There are two sides to every story."

He took her arm as they passed over large, flat gray stones slippery with foam, and he was pleased when she didn't resist. "I suppose you're going to tell me he didn't want to eat Little Red Riding Hood."

"Oh, he wanted to eat her, all right, but she wanted it just as much as he did."

"Quint!"

"What?"

"You're disrespecting fairy tales."

"All I'm saying is the chick liked red hoods."

Jorgie's face colored. He loved making her blush.

"Look," she said, changing the subject the way she always did when he made her uncomfortable. "There are the ruins of the penal colony."

Up ahead, near a copse of cypress trees, lay a rubble of weathered gray stone. They spent the next few minutes exploring while Jorgie read from the guidebook. "In the sixteenth century, the prison housed over two hundred men."

The day was warm and sunny, but somehow that served to make the location even more eerie. Dark men had seen dark days here once. They'd lived and died here on this spot where he and Jorgie now gazed curiously, with no real inkling of what had gone on. Pushing the thought away, Quint asked, "You hungry?"

"Starved."

"Let's eat."

"Where at?"

"Underneath the cypress trees?"

"Good spot."

They had to climb a small hill to reach the trees, but once they were there, they could look down on the ruins and see that on the other side lay a field of colorful wildflowers. Quint spread out the blanket they'd brought with them, remembering another picnic, another blanket, and he chuckled.

"What are you smiling about?"

"Our last outing together."

"Fun on the rooftop."

"Indeed."

"You know," she said, "I hadn't been on a picnic since I was kid, and now with you, I go on two within a week."

"Does it make you want to go on picnics with me all the time?"

She looked wistful. "Don't tease me, Quint."

"I'm not teasing."

"I know I'm just a summer romance for you. Don't pretend that we'll be seeing each other after this is over."

"Jorgie…" He reached out to her, not sure what he was going to say, not sure what he was feeling. He suddenly had a fantasy of them. A couple. Married. Kids. The whole nine yards. Celebrating their fiftieth wedding anniversary together. It scared him, that feeling. He'd never had it before and he didn't know what it meant.

"Honestly, that's a good thing. I'm not ready for anything more than a summer fling. But you're perfect for that, Quint." She leaned over to kiss him on the cheek. "Thanks for showing me a good time."

He wanted to be closer to her. To hold her like he'd held her last night. Not to have sex—although he wanted that, hell, yeah—but to hold her in his arms and listen to the steady beating of her heart.

"Oh, look," she said, pulling food from the basket, already letting go of him, already on to the meal. "Roasted chicken and cold pasta salad."

He felt unhappy and restless, but he tried not to show it as she handed him a napkin, plastic utensils and a paper plate. He said something he thought was funny, but he couldn't hear his own voice, his mind was humming so loudly with thoughts he'd never had before. *I want to know her better. I want to see her after this is over. I want her in my life for a long, long time.* What he said must have been funny, though, because she laughed gaily and the sound warmed him from the inside out.

They ate, but he didn't taste anything. His eyes were too full of her. He noticed everything. The way her chin softened when she smiled. How her blue eyes shimmered like a mountain stream, how her hair ruffled lightly in the breeze. He admired the curve of her breasts underneath the crisp cotton material of her dress, and he loved the way she'd hitch up the strap on her shoulder whenever it slipped down. Her movements were so graceful, feminine, and she captivated him completely.

They sipped wine and talked for a long time. About their families, her job, his adventures. They talked about music and learned they both really liked the sound of Texas roadhouse blues—vintage Stevie Ray Vaughan, Smokin' Joe Kubek, Johnny Winter and Delbert McClinton, as well as the cutting-edge sounds of newer artists such as the Screamin' Armadillos. The sun slipped from high in the sky, sliding down toward the western horizon. Quint was feeling content and at peace.

"This has been so nice," Jorgie said. "I really hate to leave."

"I enjoyed it, too."

"You do know how to show a girl a good time, Quint Mason."

"I try my best."

She smiled coyly and started gathering up the ravages of their picnic and tucking it into the basket. He helped her, then folded up the blanket and tucked it under his arm.

"You didn't make a move on me," she said as they walked down the hill together. "How come you didn't make a move on me?"

"You didn't make one on me."

They skirted the ruins, headed toward the beach. "Did you want me to make a move on you?"

"Honestly, I was having such a good time I wasn't thinking about sex."

"You expect me to believe that?"

"Okay," he admitted, "I was thinking about sex but I didn't want to spoil the fun we were having."

"Dumb man. We could have been having even more fun if you'd just made a move. What happened to Casanova?"

"What happened to Lady Evangeline?"

She cocked a hand on her hip and furrowed her brow. "Do you always do that?"

"Do what?"

"Answer a question with a question."

"Not always, no."

"Maybe it's better this way," she said. The grass crinkled softly beneath their feet.

"Maybe what's better this way?'

"The fact that we didn't make love. Neither one of us has anything to regret."

He stopped walking.

She kept on for a few steps, then halted, looked back over her shoulder. "What is it?"

"Jorgie, I would never regret making love to you." His voice sounded completely heartfelt even to his own ears. He meant every word.

A tiny noise escaped her lips. An expression that he couldn't decipher crossed her face. "Oh," she said, "you are good."

"I'm not just flattering you."

"Right." She turned back, hurried a few paces ahead of him, then stopped again. "Where's our boat?"

He pulled up beside her. "It's right…"

But the boat wasn't right there.

With a grunt of concern, he went to the place where they'd beached the boat; the spot where he distinctly remembered tying it up lay empty. Not only that, but the rope that he'd used to tie it up with had been cut.

Not wanting Jorgie to see it and grow alarmed, he quickly stuffed the piece of severed rope into the picnic basket.

Clearly someone had been here. Someone who wanted to keep them stranded.

JORGIE PACED the beach while Quint pulled out his cell phone to call the resort for help. She scanned the lagoon looking for signs of their errant boat, but she saw nothing except the seagulls winging their way overhead.

"I can't get a signal," he said.

"You're joking, right? Please tell me you're joking."

He shook his head. "I'm not joking. Go ahead and try your cell phone. Maybe you've got better service out here."

"I can't. I left my cell phone in my bag in the boat. We're stuck here." A bubble of panic started to rise in her, but she tamped it down.

"It's okay," Quint soothed. "When we don't come back to the villa they'll know something is wrong and they'll send someone after us."

"But how long is that going to take? It might be midnight before they figure out we're not there."

"It might," he acknowledged.

"You're saying we might have to spend the night here? On a deserted island that's haunted."

"I thought you didn't believe in ghosts."

"I don't, but it's a little easier to be brave in the daylight, when you have a boat to sail away in."

"It'll be all right. We still have plenty of food. We can take shelter in the ruins. I'll start a fire. We'll make a camping trip out of it."

She smiled at him, appreciating his optimistic attitude in a crisis. "You really should open a lemonade stand," she said. "The way you can deconstruct those lemons."

"Yeah, well, life's too short to dwell on the things you can't control. Come on," he said, "let's head back to the ruins."

By sundown Quint had a fire going to provide them with light after dark. She was grateful for the warmth, as well. Her thin cotton sundress didn't do much to ward off the cool night breeze rolling in off the water. They ate another round of roast chicken and drank the rest of the wine. After that, they sat on the blanket, their backs against the remains of the stone wall that had once formed a prison. There was no roof overhead. The fire lay just beyond their feet.

"Charades, twenty questions, or truth or dare?" Quint asked.

"Huh?" Jorgie didn't meet his eyes. She was doing everything she could to quell the urge to kiss Quint. The less she gazed deeply into his sultry eyes, the better.

"Charades, twenty questions, or truth or dare?" he repeated, tossing a fresh log of wood on the fire. It snapped, crackled, danced higher.

"You want to play a game?"

He spread his arms wide, tilted his head up at the star-filled sky. "We're stuck here until morning. Might as well do something to pass the time."

"I've never been very good at games."

"Well, sweetheart," he said, leveling his sexiest devil-may-care look at her. "It's time your luck changed."

She wasn't in any condition to watch him acting out movie titles, his muscular good-looking body moving fluidly about, and the thought of truth or dare scared the pants off her. She chose the lesser of three evils. "Twenty questions."

He sat down beside her, although a couple of feet away. "You want to go first?"

"You start."

"Okay," he said.

"Animal, vegetable or mineral?" she quizzed.

"Hmm, I'm not sure. Vegetable, I guess."

"Can I put it in my mouth?"

A knowing smile tipped the corner of his lips. "Yes, you can."

"Hey, hey." She snapped her fingers. "Keep it clean."

"It is clean."

"Oh," she said feeling equal parts disappointment and relief that his item wasn't X-rated. "But is it a little risqué?"

"Yes." He leveled a playful glance her way.

"Does it have anything to do with the bedroom?"

He nodded.

"Do you wear it to bed?"

"I hope so." He wriggled his eyebrows suggestively.

"Is it made out of silk?"

"No."

"Cotton?"

"Nope."

"Edible underwear," she guessed.

"Dammit. How did you get that so fast? That was only…" He paused, counted back on his fingers. "You only used seven questions. You're good."

"Not really," she said. "I just understand the binary search algorithms."

"The what?"

"It's simple probability, measurable by Shannon's entropy statistics."

"Huh?" he repeated. "Who's Shannon?"

"I'm sure you want me to skip the detailed mathematical description. Let's just say that if you know a little bit about statistics, you know what kind of questions to ask. Plus, considering that the average male thinks of sex every six seconds, it wasn't too difficult to determine you were thinking about edible panties. Because you are far from average, Quint Mason, I'm betting you think about sex every three seconds." She stroked her chin with a thumb and index finger. "I'm guessing cherry-flavored."

His mouth dropped open. "How in the hell do you do that?"

"Please. Do you think I'm dumb? Cherry has other connotations besides fruit flavoring."

"You're saying I'm predictable."

"Uh-huh." She nodded smugly. "But I will admit to a secret weapon."

"Aha. I knew it. You're psychic."

"Not quite." She laughed. "My family used to play this game on long car trips."

"No fair. I've been hustled. And you said you were no good at games."

"We're all good at something. You're good at seduction. I'm good at statistics."

"Not just good, you're a phenom. Remind me to take you to Vegas some time. We'd kick ass at twenty-one."

"That's about counting cards. Different game."

"Yeah, but they both revolve around that mathematical mumbo jumbo."

She laughed again.

"What? You think my poor mathematical skills are a laughing matter? Seriously, I wouldn't have gotten through college without Ashley Sue—" He waved. "But you don't want to hear about my old girlfriends."

"I don't," she agreed.

"How about a little truth or dare?"

"I don't know how to play."

"It's simple. If you pick truth, you have to be honest about whatever question I ask you. If you pick dare, you have to do whatever I dare you to do."

"I'm not sure about this."

"Oh yeah, you're Miss All That when it comes to a game you're good at, but when it comes to something I could best you at, you're backing off," he teased.

"Okay fine, truth."

"How old were you the first time you had sex?"

"Hey!" She swatted his arm. "That's personal."

"That's the point of truth or dare."

She blew out her breath. "For your information, it was my sophomore year in college. So I was nineteen."

"Late bloomer."

"Not really. I just didn't believe in sleeping with someone I didn't care about."

"You're more likely to get hurt that way."

"When it comes to love, you're going to get hurt one way or the other."

"I've never been hurt by love."

"No," she said. "But I'm guessing you've broken a lot of hearts."

"I hope not." His eyes were solemn. "I've always made it clear I'm not a long-haul kind of guy."

"You're talking the difference between the heart and the mind." She leaned forward to poke the fire with a stick, more to hide her face from him in the shadows than to stir the embers.

"It's your turn," he said.

"Truth or dare?" she asked, turning her head so she could see his eyes.

"Truth."

"What are you so afraid of when it comes to loving relationships?"

"Who says I'm afraid?"

"You did. You said you never gave your heart away to anyone. You're almost thirty. That's just weird. And come on, let's face it. You make your living playing Casanova. Clearly you identify with the guy."

"You wanna know the truth?"

"Um, this is truth or dare."

"I'm afraid that falling in love, getting married, having kids would be the end of fun and games."

"You don't think married people can have fun?"

"Not the ones I know. Sex seems to go right out the window once the honeymoon wears off."

"Maybe they're just having a different kind of fun, one you can't appreciate until you're in the relationship."

"Did you have fun with your ex?"

"That's not a good example."

"If you didn't have fun with him, why were you with him?"

"He was stable, with a good job. Smart, attractive."

"But not as fun as me."

"Now you're just fishing for compliments."

"My turn again. Truth or dare?"

She was tired of talking, afraid that he'd eventually hit on something she didn't want to be truthful about. Like her feelings for him.

"Dare."

"I dare you to kiss me."

The way he looked at her made every cell in her body flush hot. He rested a hand on her knee.

"Quint—"

He kissed her firmly and Jorgie took up his dare, kissing

him with a fervency she hadn't known she possessed. It was raunchy, boiling, mind-bending. His arms went around her waist, and he drew her into his lap.

# *14*

*A life without passion isn't worth living*
*—Make Love Like Casanova*

NEARLY TWO WEEKS' WORTH of Casanova games and courtesan teasing had heightened their hunger, the anticipation of this long-awaited event surpassing their expectations.

Her breasts heated. He unbuttoned her sundress, just as she'd dreamed he would—one button at a time, staring deeply into her eyes as he did it, stopping between buttons for another soul-stirring kiss. Finally, her dress was off and the cool night air, as soft as his lips, caressed her bare skin. He reached behind her and unhooked her bra. His fingers tickled.

For the first time, she saw that he was trembling and she realized that she was trembling, too. He dipped his head, pressed his mouth to one of her nipples, wet it with his hot tongue. Instantly, she felt herself grow wet and warm between her legs. He played with her a moment, then went back to her lips like a honey bee at a pink peach blossom. His tongue licked hers, a fire dancing in the dark.

Joy spun her head. She pushed back the thought edging up the back of her brain that whispered she was going to regret this. That once Quint had her, that would be the end of his interest in her. But she couldn't hold out a second longer. If he walked away from this night and never spoke to her again, she would let that be okay. This savory sensation, this feeling of pure playful bliss, was worth whatever pain she might suffer later.

His kisses felt different tonight. Urgent, yet tender. Bold, yet reverent.

Bumbling with urgency, she snatched at his shirt, desperate to wrestle it off him. In the end, he had to help her, shedding it quickly over his head, tossing it alongside her bra and sundress.

She sucked in her breath at the sight of his bare, well-muscled chest. He looked so powerful. Not weight-lifter bulky, but sleeker and lean. Tentatively, she skimmed her fingers over his pecs, delighting in the powerful smoothness. Had anything ever felt so good?

He kissed her again and she trailed her arm to his back, felt the strength of his spine. His beard stubble tickled her chin. His smell, his taste, the sounds of his lips on hers, flooded Jorgie with sensation.

"Jorgie," he whispered. "I need you so badly."

The romance of Venice haunted her. He looked into her eyes and her heart beat fervently. This was it.

"I need you, too. Do you have…protection?"

"In my wallet," he assured her. He stood and stripped off his pants and underwear, pausing just long enough to dig the condom from his wallet before joining her on the blanket again.

He drew her to him again. "Now, where were we?"

He rolled her over onto her back while he positioned himself over her, supporting his weight on his forearms, gazing deeply into her eyes. The tip of his cock bounced against her belly. She laughed and the frivolous sound filled the night. His hand went to the waistband of her underwear. She raised her hips, helping him strip off her panties.

He pinned her in place and took his tongue on a trip over her body, laving her with red-hot kisses. The more she wriggled, the more he kissed and suckled, nibbled and teased. A moan escaped her lips and she tried to swallow it back. She was not a moaner when it came to sex. Never had been.

"Don't hold back your passion," he murmured, his lips vibrating against her breasts. "Let it out. There's no one to hear you but me. No one to judge. Let Jorgie be Jorgie. There's no one to please but yourself. Relax. Have fun. Play."

On and on his tongue plied her with pleasure, until the desire became too much for her to stand. She threaded her fingers through his hair, begged him for release, but he was relentless, bringing her just to the edge and then pulling back. She felt like the tide, ebbing and flowing, rising and falling.

She was helpless, frantic, floundering. He sat back. The moonlight shone on his face, bathing him in a glorious light. His erection was like a soldier, standing stiff at attention. Saluting her. Honoring her.

She parted her legs, welcoming him. "Come to me," she pleaded. "Come to me now."

A quick rush of lavender filled her lungs when he entered her slick spot, his kisses pelting her face like hard falling rain. She squeezed her eyes closed, saw a bright burst of yellow sparkles on the back of her eyelids. Infinite motion, that's what she felt. Like the movement of air blown inside a glass, expanding, growing, flowing toward something monumental. He was so hot inside her, molten glass. And she was the marver, cooling him down, tempering his fire.

She opened her eyes and above his head, she saw a star shoot across the sky, blazing into the blue-black night. She gripped Quint tightly with her legs. He rocked against her, fueling the heat building, building, building inside her as she absorbed his temperature, took him in.

His body added to hers was a beautiful kind of math, increasing friction, doubling sensation, multiplying energy.

He thrust into her, the dance they were engaged in timeless, immortal. It was sweet and wet and hot and won-derful. She reached the crest a second before he did, feeling it push her upward with excruciating delight. And then, like glass, she shattered—spinning, whirling in that split second of pure, impossible wonder.

WHILE QUINT and Jorgie found paradise on a deserted island outside Venice, Avery was in Hollywood going crazy from lack of sex. Oh, sure, she touched herself, made herself come, but that wasn't good enough. In fact, it only served to make her hungry for the man in the bungalow next door.

By day, the Eros film crew shot her movie with Jake as her leading man. By night, she lay in bed pining for him. Today had been particularly excruciating. They'd filmed the love scene. It had all been covertly under the covers and they'd had swimming suits on, but he'd gotten a boner and she'd been just as fired up.

It was after ten o'clock and she was wide-awake. She couldn't stop picturing his body inside hers. Finally, she threw back the covers, got dressed, slipped into her shoes. She was going over there to tell him exactly what she wanted to do to him. She stopped in the bathroom long enough to scoop up a handful of condoms conveniently provided by the Eros resort and stuffed them into her pocket. Her hand was on the doorknob and she was just about to wrench it open when the doorbell rang.

Startled, she leaped back.

It rang again.

Cautiously, she approached the peephole. It was Jake, standing on her doorstep, looking highly agitated. Oh, gosh, what had she done to piss him off?

She gulped, took a deep breath, braced herself and then opened the door.

His eyes glittered in the light from the streetlamp. He didn't say hello. He didn't ask to come in. He didn't do any of the things a civilized man would do.

Jake simply stepped across the threshold, took her in his arms and pulled her up tight against his chest. Avery blinked. Her blood pumped furiously through her veins. "Woman," he growled, "do you have any idea what you've been doing to me?"

She stared into his eyes. The irises were a sharp golden brown. Tawny, like a lion. "I have?"

"Don't play coy. It's been your intention all along. Firing me up with your hot stripteases and your naughty little peepshows. I'm on to you."

"You are?" She felt breathless, dizzy. His broad long fingers encircled both her wrists.

"You need a firm hand."

"Oh, I do, do I?"

"You know you do."

She licked her lips. It was true. She'd grown up with permissive parents. She'd been best friends with Jorgie, who always let her have her way. She had a tendency to date playful guys who gave her anything she wanted. No one had ever really bucked Avery.

"Up until now, you've been with boys."

Defiantly, she notched her chin upward. "How do you know that?"

"Because if you'd ever been with a man, he wouldn't let a woman like you out of his sight. You need a challenge. You need someone who can keep up with you sexually."

*Oh, my.* "And I suppose you're just the man for the job?"

"I believe actions speak louder than words."

"Wha—*oh!*" Before she could react, Jake scooped her into his arms and was carrying her toward the bedroom.

It was stunningly erotic, being hauled off to her bedroom in such a cavemanlike way. It was exactly what she'd fantasized, as if he'd read her mind, knew what was in her heart. She'd never felt like this with any man and she'd been with more than a handful.

*They weren't men. Not like this. They were just boys.*

"Stop thinking," he commanded.

"What are you going to do?" she replied tartly. "Spank me?"

"I should," he said. "For the way you've been teasing me, but I won't."

"Not even if I ask you to?"

"Not even if you begged. I don't hit women, not even in sex play."

"Aw, man."

"But I will tie you to the bedposts and lick you within an inch of your life before I take you the way you deserve to be taken."

"How's that?"

"Long, slow, hard and deep."

Her body broke out in a sweat and she turned his head so she could crush his lips with hers. Instantly, she was slick and ready for him.

He tossed her onto the bed and bounced down beside her. His hands were all over her body, gripping and fondling with just the right amount of force. Not too gentle, not too rough. He tangled his fingers in her hair, pulled her head back for a demanding kiss. She met his demands with demands of her own, giving as good as she got.

They undressed each other, ripping and tearing, desperate to get their naked flesh pressed together.

Then he kept his promise, tying her spread-eagle to the four posts of the bed with her kneesocks, making sure she was comfortable, that the bindings weren't too tight, before he turned his attention to teasing her mercilessly with his wicked tongue.

He kissed her many times. On the mouth, nose, cheeks and chin. He traveled lower, loving her breasts, suckling on her nipples, tantalizing her far too long before finally…*finally*…going down where she'd been aching for him to go.

The realization of just how much expectation she'd placed on him flooded her body with adrenaline. He drove her crazy, took her breath, stole her reason. He was so much better than she'd imagined.

An hour passed, maybe longer. She lost all track of time as he made her come again and again, laving her with his dangerous mouth. And then when she was weak and breathless, he untied the socks and set her free. Then he kissed her, softly, tenderly, the womanly taste of her warm on his tongue.

"You are so beautiful," he breathed. "My beautiful wild thing."

That filled her with pride. He saw her for who she was, and not only did he not judge her for it, he actually appreciated her spunk and verve. She'd never known such a man.

Sheathed in a condom, he made love to her. Slow and

sweet. Jake was different from other men and when she was with him, she was different.

He was changing her. Sex with him was changing her. Their games and role-playing stretched the boundaries of their identity, altering their perceptions of each other.

This man was taking her places she had never been before, carrying her into an exciting but safe harbor she'd only dreamed of. A place where she felt cocooned, protected and cherished.

And she was terrified by this feeling of safety. What in the world would she do when it was gone? When he was no longer in her life?

They only had two more days together. The realization made her sad. Avery gulped. Could she be falling in love with him?

Impossible.

Unbelievable.

She barely knew him, and yet whenever he touched her or smiled at her or gave her that dark sexy look, a poignancy so sharp and sweet shot through her. Made her heart ache.

*It's because he's your fantasy man. He's fulfilled your long-held secret and now you have nothing to replace it with. That's the problem. That's what's wrong.*

Okay, so she wasn't in love with him. But she wanted him. Badly.

"Make love to me," she whispered sometime just before dawn. And she meant make love, not have sex. "I need to feel you inside me again."

"You don't have to ask twice, sweetheart," Jake replied, reaching for a foil packet.

He seemed to know exactly what she needed; he'd become that attuned to her. Nothing rushed this time, nothing desperate.

His lips carried her away. His hands cherished her with caresses. Avery let herself drift, consumed by the heartfelt sadness of it all.

Nothing mattered except the moment. Not the past. Not the future. Only now.

Later, Jake shifted from long, tender thrusts to short, quicker ones.

"Yes," she whimpered, her eyes squeezed tightly shut. "I like that. More. Deeper. Harder. I want you to fill me up. Please, more…give me more."

She tightened around him with each thrust and parry. Her heart pounded in her chest, in her ears, in her head, swamping her body with a heat so intense she felt as if she were literally on fire with him. For him.

He stopped moving and stared into her face. "Avery," he whispered.

"What's wrong?"

"Look at me."

She raised her lashes to peer up at him and she almost stopped breathing at the look of longing in his eyes.

With his gaze fastened on her, Jake began to move again. He filled her, wholly, completely. She had never experienced anything like the perfect union she felt with him. It wasn't his masculine power—although he certainly was strong and manly. It wasn't simply the estrogen dump from great sex. It wasn't even that they didn't have much time left.

Rather it was the yearning in his eyes. The solid link between them. The sensation that they were the only two people in the world.

It was all too much emotion. Too much to contemplate.

She broke the visual bond. Closing her eyes, pulling away, shutting down these feelings.

Jake thrust harder, faster. Avery mewled her pleasure. She ran her nails down his back, scratching him lightly. She wrapped her legs around his waist and clung tight. She lifted her head off the pillow and nibbled on his bottom lip.

"Almost," she cried. "Don't stop."

He pushed into her one last time, and Avery felt her sex convulse around his shaft at the same time his masculine essence shot hotly from his body and into her.

JORGIE WOKE just before dawn.

And in the muted light readying to turn purply orange she felt a sense of contentment so deep she scarcely dared breathe in fear that it would float away. She was curled into Quint, her butt tucked solidly against his pelvis, his arm thrown over her waist. The fire had burned to nothing but smoldering embers.

It was surreal, this dreamlike state, and she wondered if it all *was* a dream. The picnic. The missing boat. Their game of truth or dare that had gotten so out of hand. The unbelievably wonderful lovemaking.

*It can't last. You know it can't last. He's not a forever kind of guy. You knew that when you came to this island last night. You accepted it when you got naked with him.*

True enough, but that didn't stop her from wanting, wishing, hoping.

If Lady Evangeline were here, she'd tell her she'd blown it when she'd had sex with him. Keeping him on a string, teasing but never giving in, was the only way to handle a man like Quint.

But Jorgie couldn't keep doing that. For one thing, it went against her nature. For another, it wasn't fair to Quint. She couldn't change him. He was who he was and he shouldn't be punished for it. She'd accepted her fate, now she had to live with the consequences.

*It's okay,* she tried to convince herself. She forced a smile, trying to make everything all right. But her heart moved leaden and sluggish against her chest.

His fingers moved, playing over her skin, making her forget everything she'd been thinking. He was awake and, from the feel of it, so were other parts of him.

"Mornin'," he murmured into her hair. "How did you sleep?"

"Got several kinks from the ground," she whispered back, the cool, damp morning air demanding reverence. "And I'm very sore in other places."

He chuckled. "Me, too. I haven't had a workout…a working over…like that in years."

"You saying I gave you a run for your money."

"Oh, yeah," he said huskily, kissing the nape of her neck. "And then some."

"I suppose this means you aren't up to a little morning sex."

He pressed himself against her butt, his penis throbbing hard against her spine. "What do you think?"

She turned in to him. They were face-to-face, looking into each other's eyes. It felt so cozy, so intimate. She almost sighed, realizing it wasn't going to last.

*Don't think about that, just be in the moment.* She heard Avery's advice as clearly as if she'd been there saying it.

He pulled her closer and she held on to him, so weak with lust she wasn't even worried about morning breath or how disheveled she looked. Their bodies touched from their toes to their pelvises to their foreheads. She saw the desire in his gaze, knew he was just as turned on as her.

Slowly, he stroked her, quickly working her up to a

pitch as fevered and restless as the night before. He paused only to reach for a condom. When she was completely wet for him, he positioned himself over her and slid inside.

For a long moment he didn't move. Just lay on top of her, looking into her eyes, smoothing her hair with his hands, smiling gently. He gazed at her as if she were the only woman in the universe.

She stared back, lost in his eyes. There was no rush like the night before. This was leisurely, relaxed, playful. She could feel her own body throbbing around his hardness. She squeezed him with her inner muscles, and he let out a laugh of pure joy. It delighted her to know she'd delighted him.

Quint started moving then, pumping his hips in short strokes designed to titillate. She shuddered, let out a soft moan. Pleasure gathered, closing around her like a net, pulling tight, drawing her up. The sweet pressure melted her bones, dizzied her head, took her under in a cauldron of sensation.

He nibbled her neck as he moved inside her and she writhed beneath him, pushing back against his thrusting, escalating the pleasure. She arched her hips and he accepted her unspoken invitation, thrusting deeper, harder.

She clasped his buttocks with both her palms. "More," she demanded. "Faster."

His pubic bone rubbed against her clit. Hot friction. She groaned and so did he, a guttural, masculine sound that shot her deeper into arousal.

All the while, his lips were on her face. She closed her eyes against the bliss. To feel it envelop her completely.

She wrapped her hands around his thick forearms roped with strong veins. Jorgie held tight to him as she fell over the precipice and into her climax.

At the same second, she felt him shudder. He buried his head against her neck, whispering, "Jorgie, Jorgie, Jorgie."

In that second she knew, no matter what happened, no matter where and how this relationship ended, she was going to love Quint Mason for the rest of her life.

THEY GOT DRESSED awkwardly as dawn burst wide-open. Neither one of them spoke. Quint didn't know what to say. Sex with her had been incredible. Unbelievable. Honestly, it was nothing like anything he'd ever experienced before and that was saying something. He'd had plenty of great sex in his life.

But with Jorgie it was different. *She* was different.

And that bothered him. He'd told himself this was casual. He was nothing but her rebound because that was what she needed. Yet somewhere along the way he'd forgotten that and he'd starting feeling things he'd never felt before.

Like now. An unaccustomed misery sat heavy on his shoulders. Every second that ticked by shortened the time they had left together. Her vacation was almost at an end. Soon she'd be flying home to Texas and he'd either be here starting a fresh Casanova class, or, if they caught the saboteur soon, he'd be off on a new air marshal assignment.

Once upon a time he'd viewed working for the Lockhart Agency his dream job—never in one place long, exotic cities, beautiful women, danger and intrigue. Now he was surprised to find the prospect no longer excited him. He was tired of rambling. He'd seen the exotic cities, he'd had more than his share of beautiful women and, to be honest, the incidents of danger and intrigue were few and far between. Mostly, he was there as a deterrent to trouble.

Mostly, his job consisted of just watching people and observing behavior. That was fine for someone like Jake, whose natural temperament ran that way. But Quint was a people person. He liked action and adventure and good times, and he liked sharing his expertise with others. Maybe he just wasn't cut out to be an air marshal. He sure hadn't done much toward catching the person who was trying to sabotage Taylor Milton's resorts.

"Jorgie," he said, then stopped, not sure what he'd intended on saying.

She turned to look at him. The morning sun slanted across her face, casting her in a soft glow. She smiled and his heart did an odd little two-step. "It's okay, Quint, I know what you're going to say."

"You do?" How was that possible when he didn't know what he was going to say?

"I had a good time with you, but that's all it was. A good time."

"Um, right," he said, not because that was what he was feeling, but it was what she seemed to expect. "So you don't regret it?"

"Not at all. You've given me some great vacation memories." Her smile brightened at the same time his heart sunk.

"That's good," he lied. It did not feel the least bit good.

They stared at each other, the air practically quivering between them as they stood among the ancient ruins. Silence roared in his ears.

And all he wanted to do was kiss her again. Brand her with his mouth. Lick the hot pulse pounding at the hollow of her throat. But she crossed her arms over her chest and lowered her eyes.

He wanted to say something that would change everything, but suddenly he felt claustrophobic, as if the island were shrinking and the lagoon were rising and there was nowhere to run.

"Ahoy!" a man's voice called out in the distance. It came from the beach. "Quint? You out there? Can you hear me?"

Jorgie raised her head. He saw relief in her eyes. "Sounds like we're being rescued."

# 15

*Betrayal is an inevitable consequence of love*
*—Make Love Like Casanova*

IT HAD TAKEN a long time for Frank Lavoy, the head of security at Eros, to realize Quint was missing. For one thing, the boat they'd taken out had ended up back at the resort, neatly tied to the dock as if they'd brought it back safe and sound. For another thing, Taylor Milton had called to say she was on her way back to the villa to check out the problems they'd had with the blackout.

That was when Frank had repeatedly called Quint's cell phone and gotten his voice mail. After several hours, his suspicions had been raised and he'd gone in search of him. Even that hadn't clued him in until he'd gone looking for Jorgie, as well, and been unable to find her. That's when Frank had sent out two of his men to the island.

The two members of the security staff, Mario and Gianni, explained all of this while Quint and Jorgie tucked into the pastries and hot coffee they'd brought with them. One important detail stuck in Quint's head. Taylor was on her way to Venice while he'd been MIA with Jorgie. She was scheduled to arrive at any time.

Guilt bit into him. He'd fallen down on the job. He

knew he shouldn't have gone on the picnic with Jorgie, but he'd been unable to help himself. She'd bewitched him, this innocent-looking girl next door with a deliciously wicked side. And he was going to have to pay the price, but, man, what a glorious way to fall.

He smiled just thinking about what they'd done. Whatever punishment he received, she was worth it.

They reached the resort forty minutes after Mario and Gianni rescued them. Frank was pacing the cobblestones, looking concerned. He had Jorgie's bag tucked under his arm and he gave it to her as they came ashore.

Jorgie thanked Frank, smiled and waved to Quint, and took off inside. He wanted to go with her, but Frank clamped a hand on his shoulder.

"Damn, I'm glad you're okay," Frank said. "What happened?"

Quickly, Quint told him what had transpired on the island the previous day in regard to the boat going missing. He rummaged through the picnic basket for the severed rope and passed it over to head of resort security.

"It was cut," Frank said flatly.

"Yep."

"Someone wanted to make sure you were stranded and kept out of the way."

"Looks like it. Did anything happen last night while I was out of commission?"

Frank shook his head. "Nothing I'm aware of."

Quint stroked his jaw with his thumb and forefinger. "This is fishy."

"It is."

"How are things this morning?"

"Quiet. It's Sunday. Most people are sleeping in or they're at the festival in the Piazza San Marco."

"I've got a bad feeling about this. Like there's more sabotage in the offing."

"Me, too. I called in everyone on their day off. We're loaded for bear."

"That's good. When's Taylor scheduled to arrive?"

Frank consulted his watch. "Within the next hour."

"With all your staff on board that gives us just enough time to do a sweep of the place."

"What exactly are we looking for?" Frank asked.

Quint met his gaze. "Any and all signs of trouble."

WHILE QUINT WAS TALKING to Frank, Jorgie entered the lobby just as her cell phone rang. She was tempted to let it go to voice mail and call Avery back later, but she wanted to tell her what had happened on the island and get her advice on how to handle her feelings. She plunked down on a plush sofa in the lobby and flipped open her phone. A quick glance inside her bag told her that all her belongings were intact. "What time is it in L.A?" she asked, instead of saying hello.

"I'm nine hours behind you," Avery answered.

"So it's after midnight where you are. What's up?"

"You're not going to believe this."

She could hear something different in her friend's voice. Something reverential, sacred. "What's happened?"

"Are you sitting down?"

"Yes."

"I'm in love," Avery squeaked.

That was the last thing on earth Jorgie ever expected her friend to say. "What?"

"Oh, Jorgie, I never knew it could feel this way. It's wonderful, breathtaking. I feel like a new person. I feel like the world is wide-open with possibilities. I feel…"

She paused, inhaled audibly. "I feel so much I can't express it all."

Jorgie bit down on her bottom lip to keep it from trembling. She knew how it felt, too. Except her joy was colored with darkness because she knew she loved in vain. "What's his name?" she asked, trying to be happy for her friend even though her world was crumbling.

"It's Jake, and he's magnificent." Then she was off, chatting rapidly about the Eros cameraman who'd captured her heart. "So how are things with you and Quint?" Avery finally asked.

"Fine," Jorgie said, no longer wanting to ask Avery how she handled casual sex that had backfired miserably.

"Did you guys hook up?"

"We did."

"How do you feel?"

A mass of emotions tangled up in Jorgie like short-circuiting wires. She didn't think she could talk about it without crying. "Look, Avery, can I call you back?"

"Sure, sure, but make it much later. I'm going back to bed and waking Jake up for another round of red-hot sex."

"Enjoy yourself."

"You know I will."

"Good night," Jorgie murmured, and hung up the phone. She stuffed it back into her tote, grabbed her key card from the side pocket of the bag and headed for her room. She couldn't wait to get into the shower, where she could have a good, long, hot, wet sobfest.

Jorgie was so into her mental merry-go-round she wasn't paying much attention when she slipped her key card through the lock-release mechanism in the door handle. She barely had the door open. Her head was down and she didn't see the danger lurking.

One minute she was on her feet thinking about Quint and her life and the fork in the road she was facing and suddenly...*bam!* She was lying on the cool marble tile watching someone dressed all in black and wearing a black ski mask step over her body and sprint out the door.

It took a second or two for her mind to register what had just happened.

Someone had been in her room.

She lay there on the floor, head throbbing, fear pressing down hard on her lungs, squeezing out the delayed sound of the scream she hadn't even known she'd screamed.

JORGIE!

Quint was headed for the elevators when he heard the scream that chilled his blood, and he just knew it was Jorgie. Something terrible must have happened to her.

*Get to her now.*

Immediately, instinct and training had him rushing for the hallway just as a figure in black barreled past him and ran into the lobby. Several of the guests gasped and muttered words of exclamation as the person spun through the crowd lined up for the registration desk.

Normally, Quint would have instantly given chase, but one thought gave him pause. Jorgie might be hurt and needing him. For a split second he hung on the horns of indecision. Go after the suspicious-looking character in black or make sure Jorgie was okay?

Assuming the person in the ski mask had indeed assaulted Jorgie, then if he was down here he could do her no more harm. But what if he'd already hurt her?

"Stop!" Quint commanded.

To his surprise, the figure in black halted, but only for

a fleeting moment. Then the person turned and fled through the side door, knocking over an elderly woman in the process.

Quint's instincts urged him to give chase. Cops and robbers had been his favorite game as a child. But the thought of Jorgie lying hurt and bleeding obscured everything else.

He'd never been in a position like this. Having to choose duty over a loved one.

*Loved one.* The words etched into his brain.

If he hurried he could catch the guy. *Move, go.*

He wished he had his duty weapon. He'd left it behind when he'd gone on the picnic with Jorgie. Another dumb move in a long line of dumb moves.

Quint charged back toward Jorgie's room. He should have gone to her immediately. If anything had happened to her he'd never forgive himself. Catching the saboteur was incidental when compared to her safety. Her door was closed. Fear knotted his throat.

"Jorgie!" He pounded furiously.

She wrenched the door open so quickly, he tumbled forward, staggering across the threshold. Her eyes were wide, her bottom lip trembling. In an instant he saw what troubled her. The room was trashed. Her clothes strewn about, drawers pulled open, the covers stripped from the bed.

"A ma-man," she stammered, "was in my room."

He grabbed her by the shoulders. "Are you all right?"

She nodded mutely.

Now he raced to the lobby, flew out the side door and burst out onto the narrow. He stopped, looked right, then left. Which way had the intruder gone?

If he went right, the walkway circled back around to the front entrance of the resort. Frank's men, Mario and

Gianni, were stationed out there. The intruder would head
left toward the Piazza San Marco, where he could shed his
ski mask and quickly be lost in the crowd of tourists.

Just as he thought it, he spied a black ski mask hanging
half out of a trash receptacle. He stopped long enough to
grab it and stuff it into his back pocket. His optimism
plummeted, but he kept running, hoping against hope that
somehow he could find the man. He elbowed aside a pack
of teens engaged in horseplay and dodged a man on stilts
juggling orange glowing balls. The air was ripe with
Sunday-morning-in-Venice-during-tourist-season smells—
fresh baked bread, roasted turkey legs, spicy steak-on-a-
stick.

Across the piazza he spied a man in black moving
swiftly through the throng and Quint's gut told him that
was his quarry. The years he'd spent in Venice gave him
an advantage. The man was headed for a church, aiming
to slip through it to the waterway beyond, but Quint knew
a shortcut. He turned back the way he'd come, slipping
down a narrow side street that exited on the other side of
the church. Fewer people were here. It was easier to run.

He reached the canal on the other side of the piazza just
as the man emerged from the church, heading in the
opposite direction from Quint. He poured on the leg
power, running as fast as he could.

The intruder wasn't expecting it, but he must have heard
Quint's footsteps because he started running, too. But he
was too late. Like a cheetah bringing down a gazelle,
Quint was on him, grabbing the man around the shoulders,
taking him to the ground. The force of the momentum sent
them both flying and they stopped on the edge of the
street, inches from falling into the canal. Quint drew back
his fist, ready to fight if the guy was so inclined.

"Don't hit me, don't hit me." The man raised his hands to shield his face.

Quint stopped. He knew him.

It was Joe Vincent from his Casanova class.

QUINT HAULED Joe back to the resort by the scruff of his neck. They were at the front door just as Taylor Milton and Dougal disembarked from their vaporetto. "Here's your saboteur," he announced.

Cool as always, Taylor simply raised an eyebrow. "Good job, Mr. Mason."

They stepped into the lobby to a chorus of complaints. People were at the front desk, angry because their rooms had been ransacked. Quint spied Jorgie in line; her pale face turned his stomach. It was all he could do not to go to her. Her eyes widened when she saw he had handcuffs on Joe Vincent.

"Give me a second, fellows," Taylor said, and stopped by the desk. "Everyone whose room has been ransacked will get a voucher for a free Eros vacation."

A cheer went up from the disgruntled group and all the grumbling stopped.

She nodded to Quint and Dougal. "This way."

They hustled Joe Vincent into the office Taylor used when she was in town.

"Have a seat," Dougal said, and shoved Joe none too gently into the chair across from Taylor's desk.

Quint told them what had happened.

"You can't prove nothin'," Joe said petulantly.

He tried to get to his feet, but Quint planted him back in his chair. "We've got the ski mask with your DNA on it and we have a witness who caught you coming out of her room. You might as well come clean."

Taylor leaned back in her chair, steepled her fingertips and shot him a steady glare. "Why have you been sabotaging my resorts, Mr. Vincent?"

Joe said nothing.

"This is serious business," she said. "That bomb in Japan could have hurt someone if it had gone off."

"Hey," Joe snarled, "that wasn't me."

"But the incidents here in Venice?" Taylor waved a hand at their surroundings. "That was you?"

Joe just shrugged.

"And the threatening letters and e-mail?"

He shook his head.

"Are you working for someone else?" Dougal asked.

Joe said nothing, but sweat beaded his forehead.

"Okay, if you want to go down for someone else's crime, fine by me. I'll call the local police." Dougal picked up the receiver.

"Wait."

Dougal paused.

"I'm just the hired help," Joe admitted. "I get instructions, I do what I'm told."

"Who hired you?" Taylor demanded, getting to her feet and splaying her palms on the desk. She looked pretty damn formidable.

"I want full immunity," Joe said. "I tell you who hired me and I walk."

Dougal looked at Taylor and nodded. Taylor sat back down. "Very well. If we can validate your accusation and you agree to testify against the person who hired you, I won't press charges. But I want a name and I want it now."

Joe swallowed, nodded. "Okay."

"The name?" Taylor crooked her finger in a cough-it-up gesture.

"General Charles Miller."

Taylor blinked. A flicker of surprise passed over her face but she quickly recovered. "Cut the crap."

"I'm not kidding," Joe said, then he rattled off the times and places he'd been contacted by the general and the things he'd been asked to do. "He hired other people for the other resorts. I was only one of four." He told them everything he'd done at the resort, including causing the blackout and ransacking the guests' rooms. He also confessed to following Quint and Jorgie to the island and stealing their boat.

Taylor looked completely unsettled. "But why would General Miller do that? He was my father's best friend. He and his wife are my godparents."

Joe shrugged again. "He told me he hated what you'd done to your father's airline. That your old man would be ashamed. He wanted to scare you into closing down the resorts. That's all I know."

Taylor slumped in her chair. Quint could see the betrayal in her eyes. She put a hand over her mouth. Then she picked up the phone and made a call. "Hello, Mitzi? It's Taylor. Is Chuck there? Yes, I realize it's the middle of the night, but this is important."

A long moment of silence passed. No one said anything.

"Chuck," her voice came out sounding tight. Quint found himself feeling really sorry for her. "This is Taylor. I have someone here who's leveled a serious accusation against you and I just wanted to hear you deny it."

Then calmly, quietly, she told the man she'd trusted like a father what Joe Vincent had just told them.

Another long moment of silence passed in the room. Quint could hear the ticking of the wall clock. Even Joe kept his mouth shut. Quint supposed the general was either denying or defending his actions.

"I see," she said at last. Quint noticed her hands were shaking. "I'm sorry you feel that way and I'm sorry you felt the need to try and correct me. Your methods were not only hurtful, but they were criminal, as well. You can be expecting a call from my lawyers." With that, she hung up.

Taylor clenched her jaw and took a second to compose herself. "It was him." She pressed her lips together, glanced up at the ceiling before continuing. "The man was a general in the U.S. Air Force and he crept around like a passive-aggressive sneak thief to undermine everything I've tried to build."

"Come on," Dougal said, moving across the room to put his arm around her shoulders. "You need to call Daniel. He'll want to catch the next plane out to be with you."

Taylor shook her head. "No, I'm going home to him."

"I'll escort you."

"What do I do with him?" Quint nodded at Joe.

"Leave him to me," Dougal said. "You can go pack your things. Your assignment is over with this tour. You've worked hard. Take a couple of weeks off."

"You sure?" Quint asked, but even as he was asking, he was thinking of Jorgie. He couldn't wait to see her again, make sure she was really okay.

"Yes."

"Thank you, Quint," Taylor said. "Well done."

Quint nodded and left the room, feeling awful for her and grateful he didn't have to deal with the details. He hurried down the corridor and through the lobby, bent on getting to Jorgie.

# 16

*Always leave him wanting more*
*—Make Love Like a Courtesan*

FIVE MINUTES LATER, Quint knocked on Jorgie's door.

She answered, tipping him a slight smile from behind the half-opened door. He recognized the coy courtesan smirk she'd perfected in her class. One look at her and he felt all out of whack, as if he might be coming down with the flu or something.

"Hi," he said.

"Hi, yourself."

"We need to talk."

"Oh." She pulled a teasing face. "That sounds serious."

"It is."

"You're serious." Her grin faded. "Seriously?"

He rested his arm on the door frame, leaned in toward her. "Can I come in?"

"The place is still a mess from being ransacked."

"I don't care."

She stepped aside and let him in. He walked into the middle of the room, stopped and turned back to look at her.

The woman was a vision. To Quint she was gorgeous, and all he wanted to do was touch her. But he couldn't. Not yet.

"Have a seat." She pointed to the chair beside the bed.

He sat. She had a suitcase opened and it was half-filled with clothes. "You're packing."

"We fly home tomorrow morning."

"Oh, yeah. Right."

"I thought that was why you'd come," she said. "To say goodbye."

"I came to tell you I haven't been completely honest with you."

"Oh?" She tried to look nonchalant but he could see worry in her eyes. Jorgie was a worrier at heart, no matter how much she might pretend otherwise. "How's that?"

"I'm not really Casanova."

"You've got all his moves down pat."

"That's not what I mean." He noticed she stayed halfway across the room, as if she didn't trust herself around him.

"I'm listening." She crossed her arms over her chest, hunched her shoulders, drawing herself in like a clam. She was afraid of getting hurt. He couldn't blame her. He was scared of this thing, too.

"I'm a private duty air marshal."

She laughed.

"What's so funny?" He frowned.

"Private duty air marshal...*right*."

"Why do you find that so hard to believe?"

She studied him. "You mean it?"

He stood up, pulled his wallet from his back pocket, took out his credentials, passed them to her.

She looked at them, her eyes widening, her mouth opening. "For real?"

"For real." Then he explained to her what he was doing at Eros and why he was posing as an instructor for the

Casanova course. He told her about the man who'd ransacked her room and how they'd caught him. How he'd confessed to stealing their boat and leaving them stranded on the island.

She said nothing after he finished, just sat down on the edge of the bed, arms still crossed over her chest, still shutting him out. "That's terrible. That's got to be such a shock for Taylor. Finding out the man she trusted would betray her like that."

"She's tough and she's got a lot of good friends. She'll survive."

Jorgie took a deep breath, rubbed her palms along her upper thighs. She was wearing black workout pants and they clung snugly to her curvy thighs and he couldn't help staring. "Why are you telling me all this?"

"Because I wanted to be honest with you. I couldn't tell you before because of my job, but still, I wanted you to know."

"You didn't need to do that. I'll be gone tomorrow and we'll probably never see each other again."

It was a startling declaration for him. The thought of never seeing her again. She watched him as if he were the saddest movie she'd ever seen.

"I want us to date."

She shook her head.

"No?" Why was his throat constricting so tightly?

"I don't think that would be a very good idea." She stood up, picked up a pair of slacks that were lying on the bed. She folded them up, tucked them in the suitcase.

He suddenly felt panicky. Like he had in college when he'd overslept after partying too hard and missed his math final his senior year. He'd been terrified his professor wasn't going to let him take a make-up exam, but he'd given her the patented Mason grin and she'd relented. He tried it now with Jorgie. "Let's talk about this."

"There's nothing to talk about. I knew when I made love with you I'd already lost you. You're only fascinated with me because I'm telling you goodbye."

"That's not true," he protested. Was it? No one had ever dumped him before. Either the partings had been mutual, or he'd been the one to break off the relationship, usually just before things started to turn serious.

"Honestly, a relationship with you would be too exhausting. Playing games is fun, but at some point you have to put the fantasies aside and get on with real life. You've never left the playground, Quint. And that's okay. It's who you are. I accept it. That's why I'm saying goodbye."

She spoke lightly, matter-of-factly, but he heard the resentment and sheepishness hidden underneath. It hurt to think he'd caused her to feel this way.

He rubbed his jaw. "Jorgie, I'm sorry. I never—"

"Don't apologize," she said brusquely. "That's like a zebra apologizing for being striped. I knew what I was getting into. This is my fault."

"It's no one's fault. There's nothing wrong."

She shot him a look that withered his soul. "The fact that you think nothing is wrong is precisely what *is* wrong."

"Jorgie." He said her name softly, gave her his most effective coaxing grin. "I want to continue this relationship."

But she wasn't listening. She was stuffing clothes—panties, bras, socks, blouses—in the suitcase. He felt invisible.

"Jorgie…" He was wheedling now, trying to negotiate a peace treaty. He moved toward her, hand outstretched.

She dropped the shirt she was holding and shook a finger at him. "No, just no. You stop right there."

He ignored her command, closed the distance between them and grabbed her wrist. She snapped her hand away. "Dammit, Quint, I told you not to touch me. Please, just don't touch—" Suddenly, her eyes flooded with tears. "Let me go."

"No," he said firmly. "I have to fix this. I won't let you slip through my fingers."

"Look, this was all wrong from the start. I thought I wanted casual sex, but in my heart I knew I wasn't the kind of woman who could take intimacy lightly. I listened to my friend Avery and I listened to my hormones and I listened to Maggie Cantrell telling me how to be a courtesan, but I didn't listen to my gut that was telling me not to sleep with you and now I have to pay the price. But it's my price to pay."

Desperation knotted up tight against his chest. No. He wasn't going to accept this. In a swift sweep of emotions, he knew if he never saw her again, there would forever be a hole in his life. Hell, could he even call it a life if he never got to hold her again, kiss her, make love to her—*talk* to her.

"There has to be a way we can make this right."

"Casanova never changed."

"What?" He blinked.

"Casanova spent his whole life chasing the thrill of romantic love. He went through crush after crush, infatuation after infatuation, but in the end he was disappointed by all his relationships."

"Not his relationship with Lady Evangeline."

"That's because she never gave in to him. They never had sex. They didn't end up together, Quint."

He fisted his hands, swallowed hard. He could feel himself losing her. "I'm not Casanova."

"Aren't you?"

"No."

"Flitting from one relationship to the other, avoiding commitment."

"I wasn't avoiding commitment."

"Then what do you call it?"

"Waiting." He leveled a gaze at her.

"Waiting?"

"For the right one to finally come along."

She laughed, but it was a tight, mirthless sound of skepticism. "How many women have you said that to?"

Quint took her by the shoulders, he didn't care if she didn't want him to touch her or not, and he stared at her, hard. "None. Zero. You're the only one."

"You only want me because I'm walking away from you," she reiterated.

"That's not true."

"It's okay, Quint. You'll survive." She wrenched her shoulders from his grasp. "I'm sure any number of women at this villa would be happy to take my place at a moment's notice."

"I don't want them. I want you."

She stalked toward the door, opened it, stood to one side, her eyes begging him to leave. "You can't always get what you want."

He went to her, took the door from her hand, shut it. "Jorgie, please, reconsider."

She closed her eyes, then took a long, deep breath. He saw that her hand was trembling. Then she opened her eyes and a look of abject sorrow and remorse and utter confusion flashed. Her fragile vulnerability knifed him in the gut. Without ever intending it, he'd cut her to the quick.

"Jorgie," he whispered and pressed his back against the door. He reached out to stroke his index finger against her cheek. She didn't shy away, but lowered her lashes, closing him out again. "Do you mean to say that when we get home if I were to come to your house with a bouquet of purple orchids and an invitation to go dancing that you would turn me down?"

She glanced up and he saw tears shimmer in the greeny-brown depths of her hazel eyes. "You know I wouldn't possess the courage to turn you away. Not when you're wearing that charming smile and saying sweet things like you're saying right now."

"See there," he murmured, "see there."

"All I see is a woman too bowled over by a handsome man to get out while she had some shred of dignity intact." She pushed her hair back from her face with both hands. "Will you just go?"

"Jorgie, please. We can work through this. I know there's a solution."

"Yes, you go your way and I go mine and we simply enjoy what we had and tuck it away as nothing more than a sweet memory."

"I want more and I think you do, too."

"There can't be more. You're an undercover air marshal for a sexy resort. Women come on to you all the time. Are you suddenly going to turn into a good boy who toes the line because he's got a woman waiting for him at home?"

"For you, I think I could."

"It's not good enough," she said. "I'm tired of settling for half-assed relationships. I want a man who adores the ground I walk on. You can't help it if that's not you. Now, please, just go."

He couldn't swallow past the lump clogging his throat. She stood there, not saying another word, and for one small second his heart surged with hope. Maybe she was reconsidering?

"I'm such an idiot," she whispered.

He wanted so badly to touch her, but her expression warned him off. "No, no, you're not."

"I told myself I could do this, Quint. That I could play games and have fun and keep my heart out of it. I kept telling myself what I was feeling was nothing more than a good time with an old friend and you were like a soothing balm on a raw wound. I knew this relationship was for two weeks and nothing more." She paused, hitched in a breath, swiped at the tears trickling down her face. "I thought I'd managed to avoid falling in love with you, but I was fooling myself. You're just like Casanova, incapable of really loving anyone who loves you."

Then she snapped her jaw closed, grabbed the doorknob and opened it. "I would appreciate it if you'd leave now."

He stepped out into the hallway and she shut the door quietly behind him. Quint stood silently, cut to the bone by her comment and seared by the swell of his own shame. Her words rang in his ears.

*You're just like Casanova, incapable of really loving anyone who loves you.* And then the other thing she'd said, that thing that choked his throat and squeezed his heart. *I thought I'd managed to avoid falling in love with you, but I was fooling myself.*

Was it true? Was Jorgie in love with him?

How could a woman like her be in love with a guy like him? Jorgie should have a true feast, not a beggar's banquet. A guy with money, clout and stability who could give her all the things she deserved—a home, kids, the whole white-picket-fence thing—not some footloose guy who knew how to make her have orgasms but didn't have a clue how to meet her emotional needs.

Dazed, Quint walked down the corridor, shoving a hand through his hair. How had this happened? The last thing on earth he'd ever meant to do was hurt Jorgie. The thought of it sliced his soul. He'd partied his way through life thinking that if he embraced good times, had fun, he could avoid pain. And now this woman had shown him how wrong he'd been about himself, about life.

And that's when he knew he'd fallen in love with her, too.

# 17

*Something Sexy in the Air*
—Eros Airlines

NOT KNOWING what else to do, Quint went back to his room. He'd never felt like this before and he didn't know how to handle it. He'd just started to pace, trying to come up with some kind of plan to win Jorgie over, when a knock sounded at his door.

Could it be her? He quickly opened the door only to have his hopes dashed to see his boss standing there.

"May I come in?" Dougal asked.

"Sure, sure." Quint stepped aside and ushered him in.

"You okay?" Dougal narrowed his eyes at him. "You look…" He paused, studied him. "Shook up. This thing with Taylor and General Miller got you upset?"

"It is troubling," Quint hedged. He wasn't ready to confess to his boss that he'd violated the morality clause in his contract with Eros. "I still can't believe he would be behind all the sabotage."

"Disturbing," Dougal agreed. "I've called our men at the other resorts and notified law enforcement in those countries about the people Miller hired to do his dirty work. They'll be forced to face what they did."

"What about Joe Vincent?"

"Taylor promised him she wouldn't prosecute, so we let him go."

"And Miller?"

Dougal shook his head, sank down in the chair at the desk, leaned back. "That's between him and Taylor. Our job is done."

"The general must have had a serious conflict of values with Taylor over what direction she should take her father's airline. You'd think he could have simply told her how he felt."

"It was more than that. He was on the board of directors and Taylor believes he's been embezzling from her, as well. She's got her legal team looking into it. Apparently, he was using the sabotage as a dodge, keep her attention elsewhere while he funneled money to an account in the Caymans."

"Ah, money and greed. How often does the motive come down to that?"

"So," Dougal said, "you're freed from Casanova."

"No more puff-sleeved shirts."

"Amen to that."

"You get to go home to Roxie," Quint said.

"I can't wait to see her. From now on I'm sticking to running the office. Let you single guys take to the air." When Dougal talked about his fiancée, he looked so happy.

Quint felt jealous. "You sure you won't miss it?"

"Been there, done that, have much better things to do now. Are you all right? You look down. I've never seen you looking so hangdog. Did something happen with that woman you used as your plant? Your childhood friend, was it?"

"Yeah, that was the damnedest thing." Quint experienced it again. That hot tightening in the vicinity of his heart when he thought about Jorgie.

"What's that?"

"I fell in love." Saying it out loud, saying it to another human being, made it real.

Dead silence fell in the room. Dougal blinked at him, then grinned. "For a minute there, I thought you said you fell in love."

"I did."

"You gotta be kidding. You? In love?"

"Why is that so hard to believe?"

"You've always scoffed at marriage. At even living with a woman. You pride yourself on being footloose and fancy-free. Hell, you've never had a relationship that lasted longer than a few months."

Quint sat down hard on the end of the bed. "What can I say? I was blind, but now I see. Trouble is, she doesn't believe me. She sees me as Casanova. She won't give me a chance to prove myself to her."

"So what are you going to do?"

"That's what you're supposed to tell me. You've been down this road. You're my boss. Give me some guidance."

"Are you saying you want to marry this woman?"

"Yeah, I think I am."

Dougal's smile broke across his face. He got up to pound Quint on the shoulder. "That's wonderful. Congratulations."

"There's just one big problem."

"What's that?"

"She doesn't want to even see me."

A shudder of apprehension slid down his back when he thought of going forward without Jorgie in his life. Flying on planes from one city to another, never in any place long enough to catch his breath. How had he ever thought that nomad life was superior to the one most people were living? A loving, stable life.

He thought about his brother Gordy and how happy he'd looked with his wife and kids when he'd gone to visit them. He thought about his old friend Keith, Jorgie's brother. He was married now with a baby on the way. He saw how narrow his world was in comparison to what they had. For the first time in his life, he felt left out in the cold.

In a few months, he'd be thirty years old. How long was he going to play Peter Pan? He'd look pretty pathetic at forty-five partying with young things on his arm. How long could a guy hang on to the folly of youth?

These past two weeks with Jorgie had shown him how wonderful the future could be if he'd just open his mind and his heart to a world full of new possibilities. She was a woman who would be his friend as well as his lover. She balanced him in a way he'd never been balanced. She was smart and funny and pretty and grounded. She was the yin to his yang.

And he wasn't going to let her walk away without a fight.

"Dougal," he said, "we have to talk."

JORGIE BOARDED the plane bound for Texas with a heavy heart. *Just keep putting one foot in front of the other. You'll get through this. You'll get over him.* It sounded like a game plan, but she had no idea how to make it happen. How did you begin to forget the love of your life?

She couldn't wait to see Avery again. Avery would know what to do. Avery had been snapping her out of funks since they were five years old.

*This is more than just a funk and you know it.*

She stowed her luggage, sat down and bent to stuff her purse underneath the seat in front of her. As she did something slipped out of it. A little red glass cat.

The minute she saw it, she lost her composure, felt tears push against her eyelids. She curled her fingers around the cat, clutched it to her chest. Dammit.

She'd had to break up with him. She'd had no choice. It was better to leave him before he left her. Because he would leave her. She wasn't enough for a man like Quint. She leaned back against the headrest. Closed her eyes, swallowed hard and prayed Quint was not going to be on this flight. He'd told her he had things to settle with his undercover work at Eros. She hoped that meant he'd have to stay longer than she was.

She heard the doors close. Felt the plane taxi toward the runway. Once they were airborne, she slowly let out her breath and loosened her grip on the little glass cat. Okay. He wasn't onboard. She could survive this as long as he respected her wishes to stay away. Eventually, she'd get over him.

"Miss Gerard?"

Jorgie looked up to see the flight attendant smiling down at her.

"Yes?"

"Could you come with me, please?"

"What is it?"

The flight attendant looked around at the other passengers. "I need to speak to you in private, if that's okay."

"Yes, all right." What was this about? She unbuckled her seat belt, settled the little glass cat down on her vacated seat and followed the flight attendant to the back of the plane.

"Please step behind the divider." The flight attendant indicated the accordion door that cordoned off a small alcove area of the lavish private jet.

"I don't understand. What's this about?"

"Please." The flight attendant just smiled and waited to be obeyed.

With a sigh, Jorgie pushed aside the accordion door and stepped into the alcove.

"Hello, shrimp," Quint greeted her.

If she were smart, she would turn right around, go back to her seat, buckle herself in and refuse to move or speak for the remainder of the flight. But one look in his cocoa-colored eyes and she was a goner.

"Please," he said. "Just hear me out."

Grimly, she nodded.

He pulled her deeper into the tiny space with him and closed the accordion door. "I quit my job."

"What? Why?"

"I don't want to be on the road anymore. I'm tired of the flying, of my crazy life. I'm ready to settle down and you're the one I want to do it with."

"I don't believe you." She folded her arms over her chest in a desperate bid to protect herself.

"I know. I've got a lot to prove. But I can be patient. I can wait. I just need you to give me a chance to do it."

She wanted to say yes, but she was so afraid of getting hurt more than she was already hurting.

"I don't get it. You could have any woman you wanted," she said. "Why me?"

"Besides the fact that I'm madly in love with you?"

"Are you?" she whispered.

He took her into his arms and kissed her, firm and commanding. "Does that answer your question?"

"It's only a kiss, Casanova."

"No." He shook his head. "No more Casanova."

"How can you give it up just like that?"

"I've found something better."

"Another job?"

"Actually, yes. I've been thinking I might like to be a teacher for real. Not teaching sex tips, of course. But go back to college to get a certificate to teach high school."

"Not math, I pray."

He laughed. "No, not math. I'm thinking history. But that's not really what I meant when I said I found something better."

"No? What did you mean?"

"You."

"Me?"

"Love's a powerful force. It can change worlds, melt hearts." He pulled her closer, nuzzled her neck. "I love you because you keep me guessing. I love you because you're both strong and sexy. I love you because you see right through me. You see the real me underneath all the fast talking and fun-loving antics that I hide behind. You see the real me and yet you like me anyway."

"Not just *like* you," she murmured. "I love you."

"You do?" He looked so vulnerable she almost laughed.

"I do."

"But why do you love me? What is there about me for a woman like you to love?"

What? Was he blind to his own good qualities? "Are you really that unaware of what you have to offer?"

"Well…" He shrugged. "I've been told I'm not bad in bed, but that doesn't make me husband material."

"That's just a skill. It's not who you are."

"I've never had a long-term relationship."

"By your own choice." She traced his bottom lip with her index finger. "Besides, there's a first time for everything."

"You're not afraid I'll let you down?"

"You could never let me down, Quint."

"Really? Because here I am, a guy who's spent his life having fun and playing games and running away from responsibility."

"You didn't run from responsibility when it counted," she said. "You were in the air force. That takes commitment. And when that saboteur knocked me down, you were right by my side when you should have gone after him straight away. Yes, you love to have fun, but when it comes down to it, you've got the ability to face life head-on. You fully engage with life, and I need that to shake me out of my staid little one-track existence. You focus on the world of possibilities, and that's exciting to a literal-minded accountant like me. You're fun to be with and you make me smile. A lot."

He swallowed. "You believe in me that much?"

"I do. My love is here to stay. It's not written in invisible ink. It won't disappear if you make me mad. I love you for who you are, Quint. All sides of you. The good, the bad and the myriad in between. None of us are perfect. We all stumble and fall, but when you have someone who loves you to pick you up and dust you off, getting back up is easy."

"Jorgie," he said huskily, and drew her into his arms. "You're amazing."

"No more so than you." She stared into his dark brown eyes and what she saw reflected in those depths moved her deeply. She had no doubts about him or their future. None at all. On the surface they might be opposites—a fun-loving, impulsive man and a cautious, practical woman. But underneath it all, where it really counted, they valued the same things—romance, equanimity, tranquility. Quint provided the stimulation and she was his audience. She'd balance the books and he'd make sure she didn't get too caught up in the details to have fun.

As their mouths joined again she thought of how she'd loved him since Miley Kinslow's party. How he'd always been her image of a dream man. Now the dream was coming true. She'd found the courage to spin the bottle, play the game, and she'd won.

Fun and games had lead them here. To the deepest intimacy of their lives.

And when he slipped his palm up underneath her shirt and asked if she was game to join the mile-high club, Jorgie knew the fun had just begun.

* * * * *

"AREN'T YOU GOING TO SAY 'Fly me' or at least 'Welcome
Aboard'?"

Amanda Bauer didn't. The softly muttered word that
actually came out of her mouth was a lot less welcoming.
And had fewer letters. Four, to be exact.

The man shook his head and tsked. "Not exactly the
friendly skies. Haven't caught the spirit yet this morning?"

"Make one more airline-slogan crack and you'll be
walking to Chicago," she said.

He nodded once, then pushed his sunglasses onto the top
of his tousled hair. The move revealed blue eyes that matched
the sky above. And yeah. They were twinkling. Damn it.

"Understood. Just, uh, promise me you'll say 'Coffee,
tea or me' at least once, okay? Please?"

Amanda tried to glare, but that twinkle sucked the an-
noyance right out of her. She could only draw in a slow
breath as he climbed into the plane. As she watched her
passenger disappear into the small jet, she had to wonder
about the trip she was about to take.

Coffee and tea they had, and he was welcome to them.
But her? Well, she'd never even considered making a move
on a customer before. Talk about unprofessional.

And yet…

Something inside her suddenly wanted to take a chance, to be a little outrageous.

How long since she had done indecent things—or decent ones, for that matter—with a sexy man? Not since before they'd thrown all their energies into expanding Clear-Blue Air, at the very least. She hadn't had time for a lunch date, much less the kind of lust-fest she'd enjoyed in her younger years. The kind that lasted for entire weekends and involved not leaving a bed except to grab the kind of sensuous food that could be smeared onto—and eaten off—someone else's hot, naked, sweat-tinged body.

She closed her eyes, her hand clenching tight on the railing. Her heart fluttered in her chest and she tried to make herself move. But she couldn't—not climbing up, but not backing away, either. Not physically, and not in her head.

Was she really considering this? God, she hadn't even looked at the stranger's left hand to make sure he was available. She had no idea if he was actually attracted to her or just an irrepressible flirt. Yet something inside was telling her to take a shot with this man.

It was crazy. Something she'd never considered. Yet right now, at this moment, she was definitely considering it. If he was available…could she do it? Seduce a stranger. Have an anonymous fling, like something out of a blue movie on late-night cable?

She didn't know. All she knew was that the flight to Chicago was a short one so she had to decide quickly. And as she put her foot on the bottom step and began to climb up, Amanda suddenly had to wonder if she was about to embark on the ride of her life.

# HARLEQUIN
## *Ambassadors*

## *Want to share your passion for reading Harlequin® Books?*

### Become a Harlequin Ambassador!

Harlequin Ambassadors are a group of passionate and well-connected readers who are willing to share their joy of reading Harlequin® books with family and friends.

You'll be sent all the tools you need to spark great conversation, including free books!

All we ask is that you share the romance with your friends and family!

You'll also be invited to have a say in new book ideas and exchange opinions with women just like you!

**To see if you qualify\* to be a Harlequin Ambassador, please visit www.HarlequinAmbassadors.com.**

\*Please note that not everyone who applies to be a Harlequin Ambassador will qualify. For more information please visit www.HarlequinAmbassadors.com.

**Thank you for your participation.**

# REQUEST YOUR FREE BOOKS!

## 2 FREE NOVELS
## PLUS 2
## FREE GIFTS!

**HARLEQUIN®**

*Blaze™*

**Red-hot reads!**

HB10

## HARLEQUIN® *Blaze*™

*It all started
with a few naughty books....*

As a member of the Red Tote Book Club,
Carol Snow has been studying works of
classic erotic literature…but Carol doesn't
believe in love…or marriage. It's going to take
another kind of classic—Charles Dickens's
*A Christmas Carol*—and a little otherworldly
persuasion to convince her to go after her
own sexily ever after.

### Cuddle up with

# Her Sexy Valentine

## by STEPHANIE BOND

*Available February 2010*

## red-hot reads

www.eHarlequin.com

HB79526